MIDLIFE DRAMAS IN PYJAMAS

Tales from the front-line of middle-age

Marie Thom

First published in Great Britain 2024

Copyright © 2024. All rights reserved.

The right of Marie Thom to be identified as author and illustrator of this work has been asserted

I'd like to dedicate this book to my late mother-in-law, Catherine.

Catherine continually told me that I was capable of writing a book and she believed that one day I actually would. She was my biggest champion. I'm so sorry that she never actually got to see her belief in me come true.

Catherine, this is for you.

Table of Contents

ABOUT THE AUTHOR 1

HELLOOOOOO! 3

A SOCIAL BUTTERFLY 5

BODY ON A RAMPAGE 31

CLANG, CLANG, CLANG GOES THE TROLLEY 40

DARLING, YOU'RE WORTH IT 54

DRESSED TO IMPRESS…OR NOT... 68

FA, LA, LA, LA, LAAA… 103

FEELING FRISKY 123

HERE COMES THE SUN…..132

HUBBY HOW I LOVE THEE 151

I NEED A DRINK...167

I SAW IT ON THE T.V. 181

IS IT ME OR IS IT HOT IN HERE?...186

THIS IS HOW IT ENDS 234

ACKNOWLEDGEMENTS 237

AFTERWORD 238

ABOUT THE AUTHOR

On the day of her 49th birthday Marie went out for lunch with her hubby and two sons. Half way through the meal her youngest son took a few strands of hair between his thumb and forefinger, looked at her inquisitively and said, "Mum, when you get older, why does your hair go thin and wiry?" She nearly choked on her pigeon breast, eldest son didn't know where to look, hubby very quickly ordered her another glass of red and calm was restored.

But it got her thinking and later that evening she realised her son had a very valid question. She Googled it and realised that, coupled with other symptoms she'd been having, the menopause was on its way. So, before a tsunami of middle-age swamped her and everything started sagging, drying up or falling out she decided to write a diary of the last year in her 40s. It quickly became apparent that she couldn't write about her life without finding the funny.

After doing this for a few months she sent some excerpts off to a publisher and was told that although it was funny, and resonated with them, she wasn't famous and didn't have a platform so nobody would want to read it. 'Right then,' she thought, 'We'll see about that!'

Marie now has a Facebook page with tens of thousands of followers and has had articles published in *Good Housekeeping Magazine*, *Best Magazine*, *Good Housekeeping Online* and *Menopause Life Magazine*. She has been on BBC Radio Newcastle, podcasts, presented her poems at *Pause Live* in London and now regularly gives talks to women's groups.

She was 50 when she started this adventure and sometimes in life you just have to pull on your big girl pants and do it for yourself.

HELLOOOOOO!

I'm a middle-aged woman in my mirror, but a 25-year-old in my head. A big knickers wearer, gin and wine drinker, cocktail lover, reluctant exerciser, delusional dancer, wife, mother and cat slave.

I constantly lose my glasses, swim with my head out of the water, go into daily battle with my thinning hair and my muffin top has launched an all-out attack on my body. I never remember to shave my legs but always remember to pluck out those long, white, wiry hairs from my eyebrows, chin and latterly my nipples. I draw my eyebrows in as they are balding at an alarming rate - along with my nether regions (I don't draw those in, that would be just plain weird!) I've forgotten what sleep is, brain fog is my permanent companion and incontinence liners are my saviours. I love to laugh until the tears role down my face, and unfortunately now also my legs.

I'm ploughing through middle-age with an array of fans and a look of bewilderment on my face. I love maxi dresses, because they cover up a multitude of bleugh, and I hate reading in magazines what I should wear at my age - nobody EVER say to me 'A-line tunic and flat shoes'! If I'm told my skirt is too short, I'll just wear an even shorter one. I love rocking a long top, thick tights and knee length boots. I'm also quite likely to pair my black leather jacket with my green flowery trousers.

I hate having to go home from a party and love the fact that I was at the party in the first place - especially if it involved dancing. Alcohol is no longer my friend and hangovers from hell have become a regular feature of the morning after. But does that stop me? Does it f@&#! I don't swear a lot but when I do it's invariably at inanimate objects, or quite often myself.
Sometimes my life is organised like a military machine, sometimes it's chaos. Sometimes I'm glamorous, sometimes I'm grungy.

On occasion I go out in my pyjama top - needs must. Hence the name of my Facebook page and now my book.

Hold on tight and buckle up - let's ride this midlife rollercoaster together.

Tell your friends, bring snacks…

A SOCIAL BUTTERFLY

Was That Me?!

Friends, ladies; friends. They complete our lives in so many ways. They offer practical help when it's needed, give us support when we're falling apart, offer us a shoulder to cry on and if we're lucky they make us laugh.

One of my friends recently came up trumps with the last one on that list. Trumps being the operative word.

Picture the scene: eight people sitting around the dining table eating fabulous food, drinking glorious wine and partaking in animated conversation. Suddenly a rip-roaring fart cuts through the chatter, bounces off the walls and reverberates around the room.

We all burst out laughing and looked at the culprit - as it was quite clear where it had come from.

Quite clear to us, that is.

The culprit however was sitting there with a puzzled expression on her face, looking at us enquiringly. She then uttered the words that will now go down in history with our group…

"Was that me?"

No love, apparently your bum flapped on its own, your arse cheek involuntarily lifted itself off the chair and someone else living inside your body relaxed your anal sphincter and pushed out a fart so loud it nearly shut the twatting dining room door!!

All without you realising it – apparently.

Your next question was nearly as good as the first one,

"Was that the cat?"

Unsurprisingly the cat looked aghast, stuck two furry fingers up at you and sashayed out of the room in disgust.

We, on the other hand, were all now helpless with laughter. The ladies amongst us thanking God for our pee pads.

What a brilliant night.

Does My Fanny Really Need a Mirror in a Public Place?

I was on a night out, in a bar, and realised I needed a wee. So, off I popped to the toilet. I went in to discover that the mirrors were angled so far down the wall they were focused on my fanny - I couldn't even see my face! I popped back out to make sure I was in the right place…yes, I was.

Did my fanny have a nice hairstyle that needed tweaking – no it did not.

Did my fanny need a retouch of lipstick – no it did not.

Did my fanny need smudged mascara wiping from under its eyes – no it did not.

I tried bending down to look in the mirror – but this made the blood rush to my head and I nearly fell over. I tried going to the back end of the room, to get my face in the mirror, but then of course I couldn't see a fecking thing. So…I ended up practically kneeling down to brush my hair, sort out my eyes and retouch my lippy.

What on earth was that all about?!

Eat not Slouch

Went out for lunch with a friend and the usual area with normal height tables and chairs was full, so we were shown to the low tables and armchairs area. Or as I like to call it, the 'lean back, loll and intermittently launch yourself at a cup of coffee' area.

We were not happy.

I don't like eating with my knees up by my ears, whilst simultaneously balancing a plate of food on them.

I don't like having to cut up food whilst trying to avoid leaning too heavily on the plate, causing it to over-balance and cascade its contents all over me.

I don't like trailing my boobs through the food whenever I lean forward to pick up my drink.

And I particularly don't like my spare tyre and muffin top nestling on my thighs, fighting for supremacy and trying to convince me to buy clothes in a bigger size.

I asked the waitress if we could move. She shook her head then tried to reassure us that the tables were new, not as low as the previous ones and perfectly fine to eat at. Then she walked away – smiling smugly. Perfectly fine for Yoda or a Smurf perhaps, but for human-sized customers? Not so much.

We looked down at the table – it didn't even reach our knees. My friend and I sat down on (sank into) the armchairs then quickly got up (climbed back out) again. In a rather exasperated manner we glanced at each other, harrumphed loudly then looked around to see if any 'normal' sized tables & chairs had become available.

No.

So, we perched on the edge of our armchairs – like stealth coffee drinkers ready to launch at a second's notice – and waited. The minute two people looked as if they were on the verge of departing (scraping back their chairs) we shot over. We politely asked them if they were going, grinned when they said they were, stepped politely aside to let them out (not too far in case anyone else had been casing out their table) and plonked ourselves down. Success.

The waitress looked over at us and glared. She then attempted to take our order without actually speaking to us.

She was not happy. We, on the other hand, were ecstatic.

Lolling in massive squishy sofas while waving a cappuccino around, without a care in the world, might be hip and trendy for the youths but the grown-ups amongst us prefer to sit on a proper chair at a proper table and not have to do battle with either the furniture or our food!

Black Forest…Something!!

I spent a whole day making the pudding for a dinner party we were going to. The theme was 1970s so I'd decided my pudding was going to be Black Forest something. I just didn't have a clue what the 'something' would be…It took FOUR attempts!

FIRST ATTEMPT: individual Black Forest gateaux. Individual I tell you! I didn't rate the sponge: it was too dry and like forcing several cream crackers round your mouth with no access to water.

SECOND ATTEMPT: a different Black Forest gateau recipe. Sponge was gorgeous but I didn't rate the tinned cherries the recipe suggested: too gloopy and squidgy. Fresh cherries would have been too hard to cut into – didn't want to run the risk of them turning into missiles and ricocheting off the walls. Especially as the hosts had just had their dining room decorated.

THIRD ATTEMPT: individual Black Forest pavlovas. I'd never made meringue before, and after this attempt I never will again. It absolutely would NOT thicken. If I'd done the 'hold bowl over your head' test I'd have been left standing in the kitchen looking like a cross between a melting Halloween ghost and a heated marshmallow. I poured them onto the baking sheet – not a cat in hell's chance of piping or shaping them as per the instructions. They went into the oven as meringue puddles – and came out as meringue pebbles.

The teens loved them as they were so gooey and, once they'd cooled, ate all 16. They then begged me to make them 'wrong' again.

FOURTH ATTEMPT: individual Black Forest trifles. Not so much 'made by me', more 'assembled' by me…

Trifle sponges – no I didn't make my own. When someone's gone to the trouble of making sponge, cutting it into the perfect size, popping it into a packet and selling it it'd be rude not to buy it.

Fresh cherries – heated and softened in black cherry jam (how clever!) No of course I didn't make my own jam!

Custard – yes, I did make my own custard. Well, I say 'make'…I opened a packet of custard powder and added milk & sugar to it. None of that messing around with vanilla pods and eggs malarkey.

Cream – whipped and mixed with icing sugar and cherry brandy. Yes, I DID manage to successfully combine these three ingredients MYSELF!

I finished the trifles off with grated chocolate and a single fresh cherry on a stalk. How stylish!

They went down a treat: Nobody gagged on dry sponge, nobody got their teeth glued together with meringue and nobody had to clean the walls. Result!

Going 'Out, Out' Tonight!!!

Tonight, I'm going 'out out' girls,
Some cocktails and a meal.
I'll need to choose my outfit soon
A dress, and yes, some heels!

I'll have a shower and de-fuzz
With tweezers and some cream.
The razor also will be used
A bloody full-on team!

Moustache be gone and chin hair too
My legs and yes, my pits.
Let's hope my face at least escapes
Arrival of some zits!

I'll check my tights are free from holes
And shiny up my shoes.
I'll search my massive knicker drawer
The 'suck-it-ins' I'll choose.

I'll then ignore the roll of fat
That's pushed above the band.
And forget they will not let me breathe
Or sit, or eat - it's grand!

I'll plaster on the slap to try
And hide the growing cracks.
The wrinkles and the drooping jowls
The laughing inch long tracks.

The pee pads will be in our knicks
And in our bags be stacked.
They let us walk, and cough and sneeze
Our dignity intact.

I'll totter out to meet my friends
And hope I don't fall down.

For sure we'll hold each other up
While giggling round the town.

We might go dancing later on
'Get down' to 80s songs.
Our age will not define us girls
To let it would be wrong.

I love these ladies, they're my friends
Don't care how old we look.
We're going to have a brilliant time
Cos no one gives a fuck!!

Girly ~~Drinking~~ Shopping Day

Went on a 'Girly Shopping Day'. It's called that because it sums it up perfectly. 'Ladies' Shopping Day' makes it sound like we'd be travelling in by chauffeur, clinking china cups together, stroking brocade in posh fabric shops and wearing big floppy hats.

We would not be doing any of those things.

We would however be travelling in by bus, then finding the nearest coffee shop for a cuppa and a cake. We'd be stroking clothes in shops that some people deem far too young for us, then going for lunch - accompanied by much wine, and familiarity with the cocktail menu. We'd then stagger back round the shops to make rogue purchases. Whilst giggling.

On this particular occasion we ended up in *Monsoon*. I've never been in *Monsoon* - I have my fave three shops (middle-aged creature of habit) and *Monsoon* isn't one of them. However, my liquid lunch had been so liquid I was convinced I was in *Next*...

In the *Monsoon* section of *Next*.

I bought a top that turned out to be very expensive, but very lovely.

The next morning, when I looked at the price tag, I had a choice...give myself a good talking to and take it back OR smile at how gorgeous I looked in it, enjoy wearing it and love it for the symbol it is.

A reminder of good friends, good times and my wonderful girly shopping days.

I did the latter...Cheers!

Cocktails for Two

Had a lovely cocktail evening with a friend. To say we thoroughly enjoyed the 2 for 1 offers in the local bars is putting it lightly.

We were sitting in the last bar when the husbands of two close friends came in. Naturally they came across, bought us a drink then sat down and joined us for the last half hour of the night.

Now, to anyone observing this little exchange it would've looked like two middle-aged women successfully pulling on a night out. When we all left together – without a shadow of a doubt – it would've been assumed we were going home to have an orgy, or at the very least a drunken fumble up the back alley. Not a euphemism.

In truth me and my friend phoned several taxi companies and begged for a lift home – with no success. So, we began the journey home on foot: tottering on our 4" strappy heels, shivering in our little stylish jackets, clutching our over-sized handbags and desperately wishing we'd worn something sturdier in the knicker department…

And our chivalrous companions? Laughing. Like drains. Apparently, our footwear was totally unsuitable for the walk home (you think?!) and if we'd worn more appropriate shoes (flat) we could've walked faster and kept ourselves warm.

Helpful…

When the Chinese takeaway came into view, we all four made a beeline for it; me and my friend suddenly found a turn of speed at the thought of five minutes warmth. We ordered chips with curry sauce and enjoyed the sit down while we waited for the food – then watched as one of our male companions frantically tried to explain to the owner (who knew him) that we weren't in fact together, we were merely friends of his wife and no he hadn't actually divorced her

We then carried on with our drunken journey – still tottering, still shivering, still clutching our over-sized handbags, still wishing we'd worn pee pads but now also trying desperately not to drop our chips and curry sauce down our fronts!

Classy…

Cheers! Oops!

I've already told you I hate eating on low sofas, well here's what happened when I tried the other extreme…

A friend and I went for dinner to a new gin bar and restaurant. There was a huge list of gins served in goldfish bowls on stems – lush. All came with various adornments floating in them: peel, flavoured beans and fruit. Loved the idea of the previous three but drew the line at flower petals – don't really want shrubbery floating around in my drink, thanks.

Having decided that this was the bar to be seen in we picked a table in the window. The tables were all high with tall stools. 'How trendy and cutting edge' I thought, until I tried to sit down…in my short tight dress. My unfortunate choice of outfit allowed nowhere near the amount of movement and flexibility required to haul myself up onto the stool. And if I'd thought I could manage it with my dignity intact, I was sadly mistaken. I had to put a foot on the crossbar, grab hold of the edge of the table with one hand (while holding the stool with the other to keep it in contact with the floor) then pole vault myself up onto it.

Once up I realised there was a huge gap between me and the table, which didn't bode well for getting food successfully into my mouth. So, I had to get back down (if only they'd supplied crampons), move the stool nearer to the table and do it all again. I tried not to make eye contact with all the young, beautiful people sitting stylishly on their stools. My friend found the whole thing extremely amusing. Wearing her much more suitable skinny jeans she'd mounted her stool with grace, elegance and panache. Had she been forewarned?!

We enjoyed a lovely meal accompanied by a couple of gins and wine. I did, however, use up an alarming amount of energy remembering to keep myself upright, as the high trendy stools had no back - simply a lip that went 2" up your bum. I'm surprised I didn't pull a muscle, because every time I started to lean back the sensation of hitting nothing but fresh air pulled me up short and catapulted me back into an upright position. By the end of the meal, I felt as though my abs had received a high intensity workout.

At the end of the evening I bitterly regretted choosing a table in the window. Yes, this was the bar to be seen in – sitting demurely sipping gin, nibbling on the stylish hors d'oeuvres and politely acknowledging my friend's jokes with tinkly, sophisticated laughter.

It was, however, NOT the bar to be seen in when trying to disembark from the high stool...in a tight dress. Said dress ended up round my arse, I got my stiletto heel caught on the crossbar, missed my footing completely and slung gin everywhere! The only saving grace was that I managed to right myself just in time to avoid ungainly face-planting the floor!

My protestations of 'nothing to see here' fell on deaf ears as every head in the vicinity had swivelled round to watch the commotion.

Not sure I'll be returning to this bar any time soon...

50 Shades of Weyhey!!

I went with a group of friends to see *'50 Shades of Grey'* and the evening commenced with a meal at a restaurant next to the cinema. The waiter took one look at us and said "*50 Shades of Grey* ladies?"

I hadn't realised we were actually panting...

We arrived at the cinema, quickly went to The Posh Bit Upstairs (this was one film we were going to see in style) and sat down in the bar. The waitress immediately presented us with complimentary nachos, chocolates and bottles of soft drink. We straightaway asked for plastic glasses with ice in them - naughtiness was afoot.

We then tried to discreetly add our contraband vodka (that we'd hidden in our handbags) to the glasses. God knows how we didn't draw attention to ourselves - the girlish giggling was VERY loud; we weren't discreet with the vodka in the slightest and our misplaced attempts to shush each other were way beyond acceptable.

We were eventually shown to our cinema seats on the back row - collecting more bottles of soft drink on the way. A member of staff brought us even *more* chocolates, which we immediately tipped into our handbags for "*Laters baby.*"

The film passed by in a haze of vodka, nachos, chocolates, giggling and stage whispering. When one friend upended her nachos and spilt them all over the floor, we cried laughing. When I picked up my bottle of cola, unscrewed the top and watched helplessly as it erupted everywhere, I had to rush out to the toilet (if only the cinema handed out complimentary pee pads).

The film finished and we still had bottles of soft drink and vodka left. One of our number went to the Pick 'n' Mix counter and asked if we could have a couple of paper cups. We quickly filled these with the remaining drink... then dripped all the way to the taxi rank. Imagine that! Paper cups don't hold liquid!

Due to passing around vodka, squirreling away chocolates, laughing at unruly nachos and exploding cola, creeping back out to the bar for more ice and rushing out to the toilet I missed whole chunks of the film.
Shame. I'll just have to buy the DVD…

Maybe Not…

Ever been to a karaoke night? I hadn't but had always wanted to try it, and one night I finally got the chance on a work night out. I was nervous about finally doing it but thought, 'I'm in a choir therefore I must be able to sing: I'm going to give it a go.'

I spent all day practising in the car, singing and dancing around the lounge and belting out ballads in the shower.

I thought it would be good to have a few songs prepared. Didn't want to get there and start worrying about what key the song was in, what range the song required and whether or not there were enough long notes to show off my prowess (hahahahaha!)

Oh yes…I was going to arrive READY.

I walked into the restaurant and couldn't believe what I was looking at. Or rather what I WASN'T looking at! No stage, no spotlights, no curtains and no space. The place was tiny.

I ate the meal wondering how things were going to pan out.

Towards the end of the meal a small collection of electronic equipment was dragged out into the middle of the restaurant - frantic setting up ensued. One of our number already had the microphone in her hand and was salivating at the prospect of it being turned on; behind her an eager queue was forming.

Slight problem…the machine wasn't working.

SERIOUSLY thought there was going to be a riot.

I quickly scanned the room for feasible exits.

At last, having sent for reinforcements to fix it – obviously the sight of wild-eyed, panting, slightly drunk women had unnerved the owner – the machine sprang into life.

Oh dear…how I wished it hadn't.

The effect I'd IMAGINED was a smoky nightclub with a sultry singer performing *Fever*. The effect I GOT was a working men's club with a drunken, oldest swinger in town murdering *Delilah*.

Hmmm…

I suddenly found several reasons why I couldn't sing after all: I could feel a sore throat coming on, I was absolutely crippled with nerves, I'd eaten far too much to be able to sing comfortably AND between now and reading the menu I'd lost my glasses. I know! Bizarre!

I decided the world would have to wait for my karaoke debut after all…

Murder On the Dance Floor!
I went out drinking with a friend,
We both knew how the night would end.

Laughter, fun and raucous dancing,
Stopping life from fast advancing.

Dressed in heels and make-up on,
Our fear and inhibitions gone.
We ate a meal – how civilised,
Excitement barely just disguised.

A cocktail first and then one more,
We headed off towards the door.
Towards the club where deep within,
Our fantasy would soon begin.

We chose a club that only played
The music from our teenage days.
The 80s (as you know is great),
To hit the floor, we couldn't wait.

We put our bags down on a chair
And ran our fingers through our hair.
Then sectioned out our bit of space,
Picked up the rhythm of the base.

Around us all the people stood
Ignoring us, we knew they would.
Two daft old ladies trying to dance
And hardly worth a second glance.

The music pumped right through our veins;
The gloves were off, no more constraints.
We strutted like we didn't care,
And threw some shapes (not round or pear!)

Our arms were waved above our heads,
(No tea for us, tucked up in bed).
We kicked our legs and twirled around,
At one point lunging to the ground!

We vogued like no-one had before,
And absolutely owned the floor.
We danced and tripped the light fantastic,
All our limbs became elastic.

No nerves or tiny steps for us,
Our moves were big and obvious.
We both were on a stage somewhere,
Just grinning, dancing not a care.

The music stopped we clung on tight,
Then laughed out loud; oh what a night!
Our faces glowed, our smiles were wide;
Two friends just standing side by side.

We looked around and saw the youth,
Who maybe struggled with the truth.
Their eyes on stalks, mouths open wide,
We simply *couldn't* hide our pride.

We fetched our bags, and linked our arms,
Then smiled around with grace and charm.
We turned and sauntered off the floor –
Always leave them wanting more.

If dancing's what you love, don't stop;
Don't leave your va-va-voom to flop.

Just do the things you WANT to do,
Have fun, have laughs, be bold – BE YOU!

Offensive Musak

One of my pet hates is people messing around with my favourite songs. I detest it and it could quite honestly send me over the edge…the edge of menopausal sanity that I'm permanently teetering on!

I went for coffee with a friend and quite frankly the background musak wasn't offending me in the slightest. A little loud to be honest, so I had to lean in to my friend and say 'huh?' quite a lot. (That's actually another of my pet hates…two for the price of one! I've come here to drink and chat, not throw myself around a dance floor like a demented, sweaty, uncoordinated, cocktail fuelled nightclub go-er. There's a time and a place for that, and a coffee shop isn't it.)

Anyhoo…everything was tickety boo and then suddenly It. Was. Not! *Tainted Love* - one of my absolute favourite songs came on - but NOT the Soft Cell version. NOT the version that I dance seductively to on a night out (on a dance floor mind…I don't just get up in the middle of a restaurant and start rubbing my hands up and down myself warbling, "I cannot stand the way you teeeaasssse!" while winking salaciously at the poor, unsuspecting waiter.)

My friends all know it's my fave song and usually get out of the way to let me do my thing. I act out every word with facial expressions to match my actions. In my head I look like a gorgeous, steamy seductress…in reality I probably look like I'm checking all my pockets frantically trying to find my keys, while suffering from constipation and a squint.

NO ladies! It was NOT that much loved version. It was a bleedin' happy, crappy, fast, jolly, hand clapping, toe curling version. I nearly spat out my tea and launched a fruit scone with jam and cream across the room!

"What. The. Actual. Hell. Is. This. Shite???" I demanded.

I couldn't concentrate on the conversation until the abomination had finished.

Finally, it did indeed stop and calm was once again restored, my blood pressure returned to normal, chit chat resumed, tea was sipped and scones were eaten.

And then…

A feckin acoustic version of *Dancing Queen* came on!!! Aaaagggghhhhh!!!!!!!!

Festival Fun…

Off to a festival? Here's my menopausal woman's essential kit list:

- ear plugs (bloody hell this music is loud!)

- painkillers (bloody hell this music is loud!)

- pee pads (dancing required, wet knickers not so much)

- deckchair (can't stand up all night)

- picnic (need to eat because nobody will want to be down wind of the farts that an empty stomach will create - and I'm not paying £25 for a soggy, limp burger from the snack van)

- cool box full of alcohol and water (I'm not drinking warm wine, gin or beer for anyone)

- industrial-sized fan (I'm sure the bands won't mind if I disconnect some of their equipment to plug it in)

- plasters (not sure my feet are up to the job)

- water face spray (a hot flush in this crowd will finish me off)

- reading glasses (is there a programme telling me who everyone is? Are there instructions? Is there some light, reading entertainment provided?)

- tent (WHAT??? I'm not staying overnight in a bastard tent! I've booked into that fancy pants hotel we passed on the way in!)

- shorts & tee-shirt (it might be bloody hot)

- woolly jumper (it might be bloody cold)

- cagoule (it might be bloody wet)

- anorak (it might be bloody cold AND bloody wet)

- flip-flops (I might want to drift around looking hip and trendy)

- walking boots (I might want to remember my age and desire dry feet, sturdy footwear and good support for my wobbly ankles)

- tissues (never any loo roll in the port-a-loos)

- peg (for nose when entering said port-a-loos)

- waterproof mat (for laying on the floor in the port-a-loos: it would appear many people struggle to actually wee IN the port-a-loo)

- MAHOOSIVE suitcase to pack everything in - preferably on wheels with rubber bumpers for when one of the wheels veers off into a hole, bounces back out and bangs into a passing person, snack stand or my ankles.

Enjoy!

A Bit of Culture

One Saturday I went to the theatre to see a musical with a friend. We do this regularly and naturally make a night of it. We ALWAYS end up dancing in the aisles. Even when it's not necessarily called for…

The evening isn't just about the show though:

- cocktail before the meal

- meal plus bottle of wine

- glass of wine in the theatre bar before the show

- wine in a plastic cup taken into the auditorium

- glass of wine in the interval

- another wine in a plastic cup taken into the auditorium, plus a cup of nuts*

*got cup of nuts mixed up with cup of wine, tried to drink the nuts, shoved them up my nose and spilt them all over the floor. Then shushed myself LOUDLY while laughing hysterically!

- G&T in gin bar afterwards

Show?

What show?

Rugby Tackle at the Ready!

WOAH!! I've just nearly had to rugby tackle a woman in the theatre toilets…and that would've been rather unseemly!

I went in, all the cubicles were full, so I stood in the middle as the first in the queue. Suddenly, this woman came bowling in, banged on all the closed doors and strode masterfully in front of me!!

I was having none of that!

Loudly, I said "They're all occupied and I'M THE QUEUE!"

"What?!" she loudly replied.

I gulped, she was rather tall and had a purposeful look in her eyes - as well as wild hair and, I have to admit, rather gorgeous boots.

I repeated my statement, quieter this time, then quickly complimented her on her boots.

She smiled, I smiled. Then she realised what I was saying and politely stood behind me.

Phew! Disaster averted. Was worried for a minute that I might have had to actually follow through on the rugby tackle!

Watch out Shops! Here We Come!

We're going to hit the shops today
We'll have some fun in our own way.
We'll start off with a civilised drink
Even though we're on the brink
Of running to a cocktail bar,
We'll pace ourselves, I know! Bizarre!
We've clothes to buy and styles to choose
Being sensible, and then THE BOOZE!
Who doesn't love a daytime tipple
It gives a buzz, a certain ripple
Deep within our ageing brains
We loosen up, let out the reins.
We'll chat for hours, the bond will grow
While the cocktails and Prosecco flow.
Good times my friends, good times indeed
On this, I think, we're all agreed

Shove it Up His Limes!

I recently went to an outdoor alcohol and street food event in town, with hubby and four other couples. We got there three hours after them, so they were well and truly oiled and positively swaying by the time we arrived. Aren't drunk people annoying. One of the husbands swooped down on me and tried to pick me up. I prised his hands away from my waist and gave him my very best Hyacinth look, hoping he was receiving the 'piss off' message I was silently trying to transmit to him.

He laughed at me. Obviously not then.

I walked over to the alcohol tent and planted myself at the gin stand for 10 minutes waiting to be served, whilst standing on wet ground panicking about the white trousers I'd chosen to wear. White trousers?? Who the hell wears white trousers to an outdoor event?!

Eventually an extra barman came to join the fray and I waved my hand to get his attention, the hand that unfortunately had a £10 note in it. Waving money to get men's attention is not something I normally make a habit of. He came over, took my order then asked if I would kindly refrain from waving money at him as he was very busy. Very busy? I nearly spat my first mouthful of gin back out! Before he'd decided to drag himself over to help his mate behind the bar, I'd spent 10 minutes watching him slowly and methodically chop one small bag of limes, carefully scrape them into a bowl then meander round the back of the tent for a fag!

He's lucky I didn't take my tenner, shove it up his limes and say, "Squeeze those, mate!"

Where the Hell is It?

A couple of weeks before our girls' annual weekend away we went to our local Indian restaurant. I always write a funny itinerary and the 'what to bring' list. I handed this out, in envelopes, over poppadums and pickles. Much hilarity ensued as it was read. I've now got a reputation for doing this every time we go away – who am I not to give the masses what they want? I'd left my copy in its envelope and put it on the dividing low wall behind me. On the other side of this small wall sat the curries and rices, as it was buffet night.

At one point my friend filled up my wine glass but had accidentally left the bottle top loosely on, so it promptly fell off into my glass. The waiter appeared just as I was flicking it out of my glass then accidentally flicking it into the jug of raita – creating a trail of red wine across it. The waiter gave me a cheeky smile and asked if that was my party trick. I replied, with an equally cheeky smile, that it took skill to flick a bottle top from one receptacle to another.

Towards the end of the meal talk turned once again to our weekend away. I reached behind me, to the low wall, for my copy of the itinerary. It wasn't there. I had visions of it sitting in the prawn curry, or poking itself coyly out of the nut pilau, on the buffet table. I asked the waiter, who was conveniently filling up the curry dishes, if it was there. It wasn't.

I looked on the floor, as a second waiter appeared and asked what I'd lost. He joined in the search. I looked under the two neighbouring chairs, as a third waiter appeared and asked what I'd lost. He joined in the search.

At the point of the fourth waiter appearing and volunteering to get down on his hands and knees and crawl under our table to look for whatever I'd lost, I suddenly discovered it – on my knee under my napkin.

Our original waiter came over and, with a cheeky wink this time, asked if that was my second party trick – seeing how many waiters I could get to look for something that wasn't actually lost. I refrained from winking back but did have the good grace to blush slightly.

Nothing like causing chaos in the local Indian restaurant. I just hope they'll have me back

Going Sailing...

A friend came over for coffee one morning – I pushed the boat out and opened a packet of shortbread.

I met another friend for coffee later in the day – we pushed the boat out and decided to have a bottle of Prosecco with pitta bread and hummus instead.

I know which boat I enjoyed sailing on most.

And it didn't involve sweet, sugar coated, rectangular baked biscuits...

BODY ON A RAMPAGE

Camel or Ewok?

Anyone else got big toe nails that wouldn't look out of place on a camel?!

I've not been able to cut them for ages…they just laughed at my nail scissors. I even tried hubby's industrial strength clippers…I could practically hear them tut and sigh…

Is this something else that happens in midlife? If it is, I'm none too impressed. Trying to persuade nail varnish into the hardened wrinkles, that have now appeared on my big toenails, is not a job I cherish.

Does anyone know of an Ewok missing its toenails?!

I Refuse to Gurn Back

WHAT THE HELL HAS HAPPENED TO MY KNEES?!

For the first 18 years of my life I went to ballet class, so I've always had OK legs. Up until recently friends often commented on the shape of my legs.

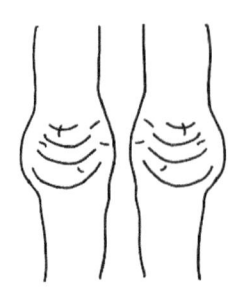

They are still slim(ish) so my 'go to' outfit is a pair of jeggings, with a long top to hide my flabby stomach. I've always had a belly, and now the menopause has made damn sure I've got a large one. It's not so much a muffin top; more a three-tiered Victoria sponge on a cake stand with a side helping of cupcakes.

But I've recently started looking in the mirror and seeing my knees with increasing sadness. Knees are functional - I get that - they hold your upper and lower legs together and allow you to bend down (something I'm frankly trying to avoid the older I get). But they also need to look nice - or at least half decent.

Mine now look like two little old men. Two little bald, wrinkly old men that have random spiky hairs on their chins, no teeth and are gurning up at me like their lives depended on it.

When I sit down and stretch them out in front of me, I no longer see knees. I see two lumpen mountain ranges with contour lines, winding paths and dry, spikey grass sprouting from their tops.

When I cross my bare legs, my knee now seems unable to support my upper leg, and feels like it's being forced half way down my shin.

I mourn the loss of my tight-fitting knees, and refuse to smile back at the two little old men now wanly smiling up at me...

Here Puss, Puss, Puss…

Let's talk about our eyesight…or growing lack of it!

I went into the hall to get something out of my bag, which was on the floor.

Crouching down I glanced across to the stairs and saw our black and white cat sitting there. Much cooing and chatting went on, accompanied by promises of his favourite biscuit treats.

I stood up and went over to stroke him, only to discover I had been chatting, cooing and promising treats to a pile of my mixed black and white knickers waiting on the stairs to be taken up and put away!

Oh, my days…

Pop, Pop, Pop…

Well ladies…let's talk air bubbles. And I don't mean the sort found in Prosecco…

I'm talking about the sort you get in a certain part of your body, where you could really do without them - your fanny! I mean seriously, don't we have enough to worry about as women without our foofs joining in the rebellion against us - along with the rest of our body? Bits drying up, sagging, ballooning, going frizzy, falling out or just giving up working altogether - I'd have thought our fanny would've had our backs! But no.

The treacherous mare.

This happened to me the other day. I spent at least an hour walking around the supermarket bandy-legged, throwing all sorts of shapes, looking like I was in serious need of a nappy change as I tried to get rid of the offending bubble 'naturally'. It's a very disconcerting feeling and I finally ended up searching out a clear aisle, standing behind a display of drain cleaner (very apt) and dealing with it manually - so to speak... calm yourselves...there were no articles of clothing invaded lol! Didn't want to get arrested for indecent behaviour!

Half way through writing this I suddenly thought 'What if it's just me?!' so I googled it. Strewth! I spent a merry 20 minutes in a menopause forum where people tried to explain this conundrum. So, it's not just me - phew, I'm not abnormal and guess what? What a surprise...it's linked to the menopause.

Words like dryness, thrush, soreness and sex were being bandied around. I quickly left the forum, closed the door behind me and didn't look back.

Looks like me and the bubbles are going to become best buddies, firm friends, or at the very least passing acquaintances because they're obviously here to stay. They seem to be making themselves at home in my lady bits, putting their feet up, reading *Good Housekeeping* and asking for a gin.

Parp!

Morning Wind.

WHERE THE HELL DOES IT ALL COME FROM?!

Am I sleepwalking downstairs and drinking six pints of lager?

Am I spending the night with my mouth open, frantically gulping in gallons of air?

Am I being force fed mounds of broccoli, baked beans and cabbage while I sleep?

I seem to get rid of so much wind in the morning I'm surprised I haven't spent most of the night floating above my bed!

The way it rattles around the toilet bowl, as I have my morning wee, is quite alarming!

The cat came into the bathroom with me the other day, and on hearing my morning symphony (played solely by the timpani, drums and bongo sections of the orchestra) leapt up into the air, shot out of the door, scrambled up the banister and was last seen hiding at the back of the wardrobe!

~~Good~~ Morning

Anyone else wake up with their face looking like it's been accidentally left in the washer overnight and dried into creases so deep no iron known to man is EVER going to get them out?!

How long does it take for your face to drop back into place and said sleep-acquired creases to disappear?

I get up every morning, look in the mirror and see my elderly mother looking back at me. It takes a couple of hours for her to disappear and for me to finally make an appearance in her place. I presume I've elbowed her out of the way and she's huffed off, chuntering about the youth of today having no manners and how old age will come to me soon enough - but inside she still only feels 18...

When I was young, I used to laugh when she said that to me. I'd think to myself, surely nature ages your mind at the same time as it ages your body - to enable you to accept the changes with calmness and grace, as opposed to flailing around on the floor like a snotty-nosed toddler having a tantrum.

Apparently not, as I now know EXACTLY what she meant!

One day she'll refuse to huff off and will resolutely remain in the mirror. But do you know what? If I'm still here at her age, looking as good as she does, then that's fine by me

Farty Pants

OMG! OMG! OMG!

I returned to the car after a shopping trip, opened the back door, leant in to deposit my booty into the footwell and let out the most ENORMOUS FART known to man! I'm surprised it didn't catapult me into the car, face plant me onto the back seat and demand a bloody round of applause! I actually feared for my jeans! I instantly exclaimed, "Bugger me! That was a good one!" then burst out laughing.

I closed the back door, thinking, 'Thank feck I'm in a car park with no one around!' then got into the car, shut the door, put my seat belt on and glanced through the side window. To discover... a bloke sitting in his car next to mine, laughing, winding his window up and sticking his thumbs up at me!

I've never reversed out of a parking space so quickly, so bright red and so convulsed with giggles!

Seriously?

I woke up with a sharp pain down my neck and right shoulder and could barely move my head.

Did I have an energetic night of sex, using positions I've previously only had nightmares about? NO.

Did I do a new and torturous workout routine, with a personal trainer pushing me to my limits, last night? NO.

Did I paint every wall in the house, including the outside, yesterday? NO.

NO!!!

I turned over in my sleep and pulled a feckin' muscle!

The joys of midlife

Ping!

Well, that's me off to bed. I've dozed through an episode of a drama, drunk a mug of hot milk, had the cat sleeping on my lap and snuggled down in my furry dressing gown.

I'm struggling to keep my eyes open.

Queue my head hitting the pillow: a shopping list will dam-bust its way into my head; witty ripostes that I should've used in arguments weeks ago will swirl around in my brain; how I'll sort out a work issue tomorrow will skitter across my mind and worrying about the state of the world will vie for my attention! And PING!! I'll be feckin wide awake!!

BINGO WINGS

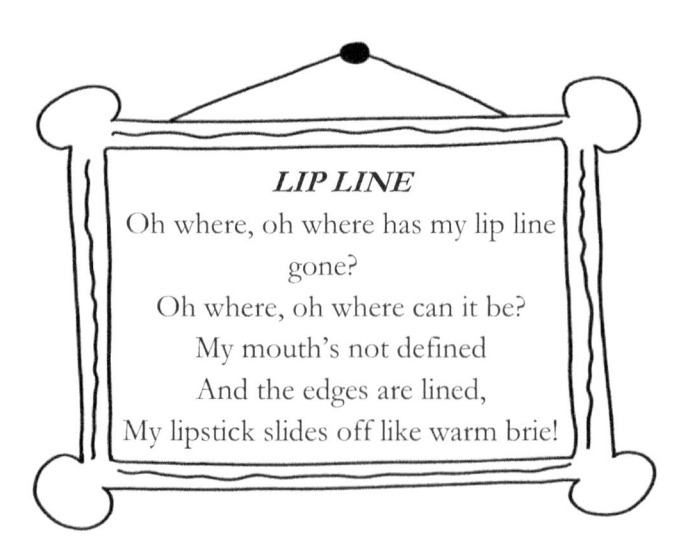

I'd quite like to know
why the skin on my arms
Is saggy and wobbly and flaps.
When drying my hair
It ripples around
And needs holding
With duct tape and straps!

LIP LINE

Oh where, oh where has my lip line gone?
Oh where, oh where can it be?
My mouth's not defined
And the edges are lined,
My lipstick slides off like warm brie!

CATERPILLAR

Just rescued a tiny caterpillar from the sink. Picked it up carefully, talked to it while moving it outside, placed it gently onto a leaf then put my glasses on to check it was ok.

It was an effin' grape stalk!!

CLANG, CLANG, CLANG GOES THE TROLLEY

She Nose, You Know

You know when you absolutely have to blow your nose, because there's something up there that needs excavating, but no amount of sniffing will work? Well, that was me. 10 minutes I spent walking up and down the aisles of the supermarket, sniffing. This ranged from a delicate sniffle - usually accompanied by a lace handkerchief, a flapping hand and an, "Oh Mr Darcy, be still my fluttering nasal cavity" - all the way through to a boot dragging snort that Shrek in his swamp would've been impressed by.

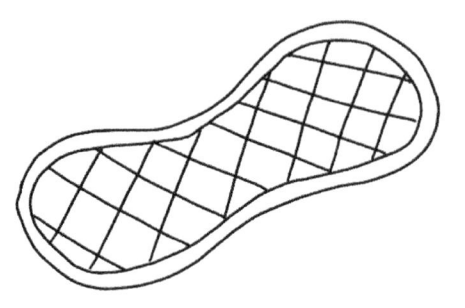

I eventually gave up and frantically looked in my bag for a tissue - quickly realising that my search was futile. The only thing I found (lurking at the bottom) was a pee pad.

So, I quickly sought out a deserted aisle, unwrapped it, blew my nose into it, re-wrapped it and shoved it back into my bag.

I kid you not…

Yay! Well done, pee pad! Who knew you could be so versatile. Apparently, you aren't fussy about which bodily fluids are welcomed into your inner sanctum, with open flaps…

Bit Nippy

I was at the supermarket and was mightily glad I did not have my pyjama top on (it has been known). It was so bloody cold in there that my goosebumps looked like someone had covered my arms in tapioca! My hairs were so erect I could've picked up Radio 2 and my nips were standing out like chapel hat pegs!

If they hadn't been safely contained within a bra, they'd have been in danger of clearing whole shelves of grocery products and poking innocent customers in the eye!

On Another Occasion…

Another time, when I went to the supermarket and actually *did* have my pyjama top on, I had a hot flush and was completely buggered.

I had a cardigan and hoodie over said pyjama top and suddenly started to get very hot. I quickly removed the hoodie and wafted my face with the shopping list, to no avail. I was desperate to rip off the cardigan, but obviously couldn't because underneath it I was quite obviously wearing a pyjama top. The cute sleeping bears and lace trim would absolutely have given it away.

So, I quickly headed to the frozen food aisle and found the contents of the upright freezers surprisingly interesting. By the time the heat had subsided I had a date with Captain Bird's Eye, Aunt Bessie had volunteered to chaperone us, Dr. Oetker was giving me advice on safe sex and The Jolly Green Giant had promised to lend me his loin cloth!

Ooooo, That's a Bit Draughty!

I'd been struggling with the summer heatwave so had worn a short, floaty dress to do the weekly shop. However, it was only when I got out of the car, and a sudden breeze plunged me into a Marilyn Monroe moment, that I had a dawning sense of realisation...this was a dress I normally wore over black leggings.

I went into the supermarket with my trolley, leant in to it to add an item and felt a rather unnerving chill around my arse. I slapped my hand round to my rear end to investigate the issue - and only then did I realise just how short the dress became when I bent over. I now had the tricky job of working out how to get things into the trolley without being arrested for indecent exposure.

Let's just say that being an expert in Tai Chi would have been really helpful.

I resorted to: putting things in backwards and hoping it was actually MY trolley I was putting them in to; sidling up to the long edge of the trolley and dropping things in seductively over the edge; and pretending I was at the ballet barre performing a plie while lowering things in slowly. Slowly because I was in fear of over-bending and toppling into said trolley!

Getting things from the lower shelves proved interesting...squatting not being a great look at the best of times. I also had to remember to keep facing the shelves to get back up again, as opposed to scaring innocent passersby when swivelling around unexpectedly.

So, I squatted and lunged my way around the shop while constantly talking and giggling to myself. I could be heard muttering things like, 'Well that's not going to work', 'How the hell am I going to do that?' and 'Dear me, that's not a pretty sight!'

Struggling to manhandle a massive bag of cat litter was nearly my undoing.

But you know what? I reckon I managed to get through my whole shop without the entire customer base of the supermarket unwittingly becoming my gobsmacked gynaecologist!

Nice Lycra, Love…

I got my bike out again; it's lain dormant for quite a while but the weight was creeping back up. I'd cycled round the village and gone into the shop to get one thing - for which I had enough change in my natty, little cycling top pocket.

So far so good…

So far so good until I decided to get a whole load of lovely salad things for my lunch. As I was adding more and more things to my basket (never go food shopping when you're hungry), it suddenly dawned on me that the few coins I'd stashed about my person wouldn't cut it with my now bulging basket.

So, I frantically rang my son and asked him to come up to the shop with my purse. I then presented a lovely image to all the unsuspecting shoppers, as I stood there waiting for him to arrive. My Lycra cycling shorts were whispering, 'Here's my belly', my tight Lycra cycling top was saying, 'Here's my muffin top' and my bare legs were shouting, 'FFS woman, if they were any whiter, they wouldn't look out of place on a polar bear - they're certainly hairy enough!'

It Won't Go In!

Meno brain embarrassing moment at the supermarket today…

I returned my trolley to the car park trolley store and found it was the first one in the line. I stopped it at the metal bar, went forward and picked up the chain with the token releasing doofer attached. I pulled it towards my trolley lock to find it was about 10" too short. "WTF?" I declared under my breath, followed by, "How am I supposed to get my trolley token back out?" and "What idiot has wrapped the chain around the bar like that? I guess I'm going to have to unwrap it, but wait! It's in a knot! WTAH?"

Enter stage left - across the other side of the chain holding bar and trolley shelter - a young male supermarket employee.

"Look at this!" I declared. "The chain is too short! It's in a knot on the bar. I'm going to have to somehow unravel it! This is preposterous!" This was accompanied by futile pulling of the chain towards my trolley handle to illustrate the problem. (I hasten to add that my tone was incredulous not cross. I'm not one of those people who takes things out on unsuspecting, innocent retail staff lol!)

He glanced first at the bar attached to the chain, and then secondly at my trolley.

"Madam," he said, and with a wink and a smile, followed that up with, "You need to push it all the way in…"

I went bright red with embarrassment at my ineptitude and laughed out loud.

Then I pushed my trolley front UNDER the bar, picked up the chain, released my token, wished him a good day and beetled off back to my car muttering FML under my breath…

Escaping Bloomer

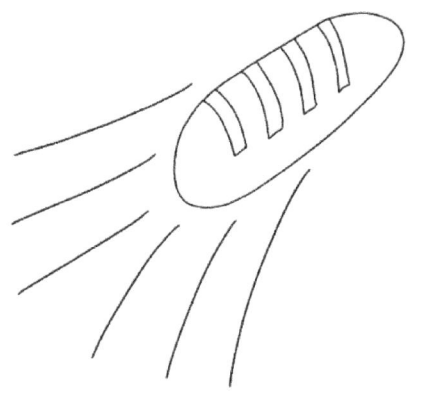

We had family coming over, so my trolley was, to say the least, packed to the rafters. I had bags hanging off every corner, and of course I'd picked a trolley with a dodgy wheel. This meant I spent a lot of time veering off into weird directions - like trying to steer an obstinate toddler straining to dive head first into the pick n mix display. Many variations of the F word were muttered, whispered, spoken and eventually shouted at inanimate objects as I made my way around the store.

As the trolley got fuller, and the steering got more difficult, things kept sliding towards the edge and threatening to throw themselves onto the floor. The transformation into screaming, face planting toddler would've been complete.

And I'm talking about me - not the trolley.

I finally finished and dragged the behemoth of shopping to the self-scan checkout. Sweat dripped down my back as I registered my sale - desperately hoping the till wouldn't request a service check. I just knew the assistant would happen upon the one item I'd accidentally missed. This would mean that my entire 4-storey high trolley would have to be emptied and re-scanned. Lights would flash, doors would slam shut, help would be required and extra assistants would come running from all directions. I'd have to stand awkwardly like a menopausal version of Richard Madeley; only it wouldn't be champagne that would be my undoing, it would be a pack of friggin pee pads!

Fortunately, I survived and none of this happened. I sailed out of the store and breathed a sigh of relief as my massive shop was done. I smiled benignly at my expert packing of the trolley, and complimented myself on surviving the trip with a modicum of dignity.

Then I accidentally pushed it over a stone, and it started to pick up speed. The loose bloomer, that I had precariously balanced on the top of the pile, saw its chance and started to slip towards the edge. Without warning it suddenly launched itself into the air and hurtled towards the ground. I lunged to try and catch it (while also trying to stop the now road bound trolley), yelped, swore loudly and bloody WET MYSELF!!

Pssssssssssss....

I didn't have much to get at the supermarket, so chose a pull along basket. I love a pull along basket and often feel like sitting in one at the entranceway, trying to look appealing and smiling at passers-by, in the hope that someone will pull ME along in it.

I was quite merrily tootling up and down the aisles, filling said basket, when I suddenly started to hear a long, loud hissing sound. I have a massive phobia of snakes. When I see one on the television my toes instantly curl up inside my shoes and my legs shoot up onto the sofa.

I quickly looked around expecting to see an anaconda (I'm extremely dramatic; it's part of my charm) slithering its way from under the incontinence liner shelves. After checking up and down the aisle I saw nothing of a reptilian nature, so assumed it was the store's heating system doing something necessary. I carried on with my shopping.

Then I started to smell a rather sweet perfume-like scent. I glanced around to try and see the Adonis that had clearly just walked past wearing enough cheap aftershave to wipe out several women, 10 small children and 15 supermarket staff.

But the aisle was empty.

I carried on with my tootling, unaware of the odd glance in my direction from fellow shoppers. I then squatted down to reach the biscuits on the bottom shelf. The hissing was instantly right by my ear and the sweet perfume smell nearly knocked me out. Both were coming from my basket! I stared into my shopping and discovered that a four pack of beans was sitting VERY HEAVILY on top of an aerosol can of deodorant, which was enthusiastically spraying its contents everywhere, with uninhibited joy.

WTF?!

I swiftly moved the beans and checked around to see if anyone had noticed. I'd apparently been walking around the shop leaving a cloud of deodorant behind me the whole time. No wonder I'd been getting odd looks as I sashayed past!

"You effin' numpty!" I declared to myself under my breath. Then I burst out laughing. I quickly got a tissue and had to wipe ALL of my shopping - which was now covered in deodorant residue and smelt like a teenage boy's bedroom just before he leaves for a night out in the hope of getting lucky.

I stood up - not too quickly for fear of a menopausal head spin - and went back to the toiletries shelf to pick up another can of deodorant, to accompany the now half empty original can.

I paid - ignoring the bemused look on the face of the shop assistant as he realised that everything in the basket had a slightly slimy film to it - and left.

I sometimes wonder why these things always seem to happen to me. I wander through life feeling like a complete idiot at times, but always manage to laugh about it. It's all we can do, isn't it?

Attack of the Killer Handbag

Just had an all-out battle with my handbag in the car park.

I'd been for a cuppa before starting the shopping and obviously taken my jacket off. When I'd finished I put my bag across my body, followed by my jacket, and completed my shopping.

I packed the shopping away in the boot of the car then whipped my bag off over my head.

Only I didn't...because my bag was UNDER my jacket!

So, what I actually did was pull the bag strap over my head, half yank my sleeve off, catch my hair and hood in the strap, flail around in a whirlwind of green puffa, trip over the trolley wheel and narrowly avoid falling headfirst into the boot!

Calm Yourself, Jessica Rabbit!

Well yesterday's embarrassment was gamely provided by our local shop…thank you very much!

I was using the self-service till quite happily. I finished, chose 'pay by card' and plonked my card on the reader. Suddenly the till shouted at me "CARD DECLINED, INSERT CARD, CARD DECLINED, INSERT CARD!"

*Red lights lit up, the doors slammed shut, armed guards surrounded me and every head turned…

*slight exaggeration me thinks

"But that's how it felt, your honour!"

Isn't it bad enough that we're faced with a cartoon character of a woman on the till display (who looks like effin Jessica Rabbit) telling us to start our shopping, scan first item, finish and pay - as if her life depended on the speed of our shopping? But now we also get shouted at if there's a slight issue with our card!

Did Jessia Rabbit's head swivel round, green bile spew from her mouth and red lights shine from her eyes?

Quite possibly.

Thankfully once my card was re-entered, the transaction went smoothly; but my feathers were definitely ruffled, my knickers were in a twist and my nerves were completely discombobulated!

Chatter, Chatter, Chatter…

Do you talk to yourself?

I do…ALL. THE. TIME.

Hubby will often come in and shout upstairs, "Who's up there with you?!"

Only me. And myself.

I often spend the entire time in the supermarket nattering away to myself, for example:

"What do you mean there isn't any ground cumin? There wasn't any last week either!"

"Who on earth could wear this dress and not look like a bag of spuds? And what on earth is that bit meant to do?"

Holding up a jumpsuit, "Well that's not going to be pleasant is it! Why is there no proper opening? Are clothes designers so above us that they never need to go the loo?!"

Trying on a jacket, "Why doesn't it meet in the middle? Is it meant to meet in the middle? It's definitely my size… and why is the lapel not creased properly?"

"Who thinks it's a good idea to have all this bakery bread uncovered? Haven't they heard of germs! Bloody hell, that bloke's just sneezed all over the split tins!"

"Why the hell did I pick the trolley with the dodgy wheel?" And to passers-by, "Sorry! I've got no control over it! The treachery of the thing is appalling!"

"I bet I get a service check...I bloody KNOW I'll get a service check...did I scan those twatting eggs?"

"OMG! The custard tarts have gone rogue...they're going to fall out of the trolley!"

"Puy lentils...where the hell are the Puy lentils? Why can I never find them? Oh, for FFS...what a stupid place to put them...who thought that would be a good place? Probably a man"

Now, you may think that all of this is in my head. But it's not. It is very happily falling out of my mouth - and not in a whisper either!

I get some very odd looks while I'm doing my shopping - and quite often I'm given a VERY wide berth.

In the Doghouse

I left the house to go to the supermarket thinking I looked ok. I still had yesterday's make-up on – contrary to what magazines say I actually find this makes me look like I've got great skin the next morning. I hadn't bothered scraping my hair up but I had at least used eye make-up remover to tidy away yesterday's mascara from underneath my eyes.

I was quite happily pootling up and down the aisles when I suddenly caught sight of my reflection in a 4" wide mirror, between the fridge display cabinets.

Oh. My. God. I did not look ok at all.

I had eye bags like a bloodhound, jowls like a St Bernard and hair like a limp Afghan! Thank God the mirror was only 4" wide. Not sure I would've coped coming face-to-face with a whole dog rescue centre staring back at me. And not a pristine, well-funded dog rescue centre either! No… a down-at-heel, underfunded, puddles of pee on the floor, lacking in TLC dog rescue centre!

Balloons, Where?

I got to the till and the girl at the checkout scanned a pack of balloons I'd picked up. The till was having none of it and flashed up the message 'Product withdrawn, don't sell on pain of death' or words to that effect. She pressed her bell to summon help, which came in the form of a male supervisor who looked like he was barely out of primary school and should be at home worrying about his homework, not the trials and tribulations of a middle-aged woman. He took the offending packet of balloons and asked me what I'd like to exchange them for. "Balloons," I said. "They need to be so big," I made round shapes with my hands, "And quite strong."

The two of them looked at me inquisitively. "Do you need a specific colour?" he asked.

"No, any colour will do" I replied.

"Do they need to have anything written on them?"

"It doesn't matter, nobody will be seeing them."

"Nobody will be seeing them?" He looked confused.

"No," I grinned. "They're going under my husband's dress."

"What?!"

I'm not sure what threw him most – the fact that my husband has a dress or the fact that he's stuffing balloons down it.

Clearly, they were both dying to ask me for more details about this strange occurrence, but social etiquette was preventing them from doing so. I put them both out of their misery.

"He's going to a fancy-dress party and he needs boobs."

The young male supervisor looked at me blankly, then quickly scuttled off down to the safety of the aisles.

The girl on the till suddenly found the contents of her carrier bag storage unit extremely fascinating.

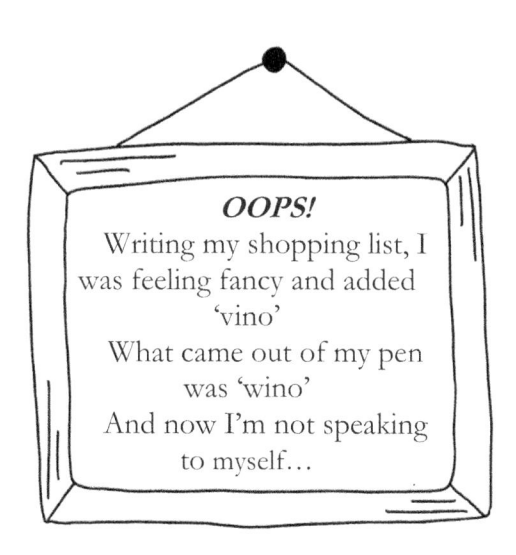

OOPS!
Writing my shopping list, I was feeling fancy and added 'vino'
What came out of my pen was 'wino'
And now I'm not speaking to myself…

DARLING, YOU'RE WORTH IT

Are You Watching Carefully?

I've just seen a make-up tutorial on *You Tube* and watched a young woman put so many different creams on her face I'm surprised she could move it when she'd finished. I was almost expecting it to slump forward onto the table, as it crumpled under the weight. I say crumpled…it couldn't have crumpled if her life had depended on it. And she looked like a completely different person when she'd finished.

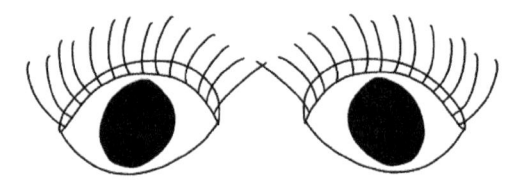

Shouldn't make-up enhance your face, not allow you to get away with criminal activity because you look nothing like yourself?

Apparently, I need primer, highlighter, blusher, contour cream, foundation, powder, concealer, bronzer, eyebrow pencil, eyebrow wax, lash primer, mascara, an eyeshadow palette, lip liner, eyeliner, false eyelashes, lipstick and lip gloss. Whatever happened to 'less is more'? It now seems to be 'more is more' followed by 'and shovel even more on for good luck'.

If you don't have any false eyelashes, stick a couple of these on…

How do these young ladies ever get anywhere on time?!

When I was their age I managed foundation, blusher, mascara and lippy. That was it. And that took me FOREVER.

To me a contour was something we looked at on maps in geography lessons, a concealer was my little sister hiding my new *Human League* cassette, a primer was a substance used by my dad when he painted woodwork, a highlighter was a bright yellow felt tip pen, bronzer was someone who'd sat out in the sun too long and a palette was a flat knife my mum used to prise a quiche off a baking tray!

Bleedin Nora!! I'm going out on Saturday night…I'd better get started now!!

Tight Teeth, Anyone?

I once cleaned my teeth in a dark bathroom without my glasses on - and accidentally used haemorrhoid cream instead.

I thought it was a bit difficult to persuade out of the tube, but carried on regardless. I soon realised all was not well and spat it out, then hurriedly swilled out my mouth - which proved quite difficult as the bastard cream was clinging to my teeth like a Liz Truss lettuce clinging onto power.

I ended up with the tightest teeth known to man - which were gallantly trying to squeeze themselves back up into my gums.

However, my gums were going "Nope. Your name's not down, you're not coming in"

It proved to be quite the battle.

To Brow, or Not to Brow.

A while ago I decided it was time I had some drawn-on eyebrows. My own eyebrows had decided they weren't needed anymore and had made their way down to my top lip and chin. Maybe they thought they'd get better working conditions down there. However, they had kindly left behind the odd 2" long white, wiry hair sticking out at right angles to my face.

Rude…

I stood balefully gazing at the eyebrow pencil selection, wondering if I was a light brown, warm brown, medium brown, dark brown, mid-brown, chestnut, hazel, tawny or chocolate. Feckin' hell!

My hair is medium brown (out of a bottle) but my eyebrows are brown shot through with white – this does not make me look distinguished; it makes me look like an aged badger. Eventually a make-up assistant came over to advise me. I finally left with a warm brown pencil plus a special sharpener – but I'd laughed at her suggestion of a tube of wax to keep said eyebrows in place. I walked away shaking my head and smiling at the youth of today.

Did she honestly think I couldn't look after a pair of eyebrows?!

I got home and immediately filled in my scratty eyebrows. I looked like I was permanently frowning; maybe I'd drawn them too far into the middle – though obviously I'd stopped short of a mono-brow. I wasn't sure if I looked permanently surprised, permanently cross or permanently bewildered. I used a cotton bud to try shaping them and make them look less frightening.

I took my new eyebrows to the pub. No-one said a word about them, but I did get a few quizzical looks - obviously I assumed these were looks of admiration for my new lush, brown brows.

I got home, looked in the mirror and couldn't quite believe what I was seeing. I'd managed to smudge one of the feckin' eyebrows RIGHT ACROSS MY FOREHEAD!!

Turns out the shop assistant was right – I DID need the wax because I am NOT ready to be out in public with sole responsibility for a pair of eyebrows!

Watch Out for the Suction!

So, shower puffs? I'm all for them. They make the shower gel lather up beautifully.

Shower puffs with a hanging loop attached? Great. Means you can hang them over the shower controls.

Shower puffs with a hanging loop, AND a suction cup attached? WTF? Fab in principle, bonkers in practice.

Every time you swing the shower puff round to a different part of your body, the suction cup randomly attaches itself to the nearest wall. I've lost count of the number of times I've moved it through my legs then tried to bring it back, only to discover it's stuck to the rear wall.

Knocking my forehead on the soap dish, as my arm jerks with the shower puff's refusal to move, is now a daily occurrence.

And don't get me started on trying to pick it up from the floor…

Smoky Eye, My Arse!

I decided that, as a fully grown adult, I should be able to create a smoky eye when I go out wearing full make up (full make up as opposed to last night's mascara, smudged eyebrows and a look of apology).

On numerous occasions I've attempted to get the smoky, sultry look – and failed every time. I invariably end up looking like I should be standing on a street corner in the desperate section of the red-light district, or propping up a bar scaring innocent young men as I flare my absurd eyes at them. If I do a really bad job, I can end up looking as though I should be draped around a pole in a Saga nightclub– having first tried to stuff my middle-aged muffin top into laughably tiny bits of lace.

So, in the supermarket today I headed to the make-up counters in search of eye shadow. The palette currently residing in my make-up drawer has been there at least 10 years and includes: bright green and blue, a worn-out brush, a cracked mirror and the odd cat hair.

I felt that powder shadow was probably best; cream tends to congeal in my eyelid creases: it refuses to blend in, ends up in stripes and has been absorbed into my body within an hour of being applied. Feck knows where it goes but it's certainly no longer on my eyelids.

I fleetingly dabbled with colour tattoo 24-hour eye make-up a while ago. The problem with this is that it won't come off. Red, watery, puffy eyes is a look I can manage on my own thanks - without the aid of a cotton wool pad soaked in industrial strength cleanser and 10 minutes of gentle dabbing (scrubbing).

So, I found a stand with little pots of testers in every colour you could imagine. My eyes lit up. I was drawn to an off-white, sparkly one. Who doesn't love a bit of sparkle. I carefully extended my finger and placed it into the pot, ready to test its suitability – only to discover that not only was it NOT eye shadow but that it was in fact BODY SHIMMER and therefore, extremely loose and powdery.

FFS! I attempted to wipe if off but it refused to budge. I tried shaking it off, and flicking it off but stopped short of licking it off. It seemed to have the staying power of a menopausal chin hair - refusing to move, winking at me with glee and oblivious to any attempts to get rid of it.

I spent the rest of my time in the supermarket with a finger nail full of white sparkly shimmer, a cascade of it down my coat, rogue specks glinting up at me from the tops of my shoes and a smear of it across my shopping list!

I finished my shopping, ignored the curious glances of the staff and left with a firm resolution to give myself a good talking to and give up on the smoky eye, love!

Are you a Bender or a Squatter?

My current pot of night-time moisturiser (night-time AND day-time?! Won't one pot do all?) is coming to an end. I've had it at least two years, which shows how diligently I use it...

I'm already using a serum which is supposed to show results within four weeks. I've been using it for four months. I'm still waiting for the moment when I look in the mirror and discover that the old hag has been replaced by a dewy-faced, glowing beauty.

According to the adverts, that's what should happen.

Pah – not in my mirror!

As you scan the shelves, you'll see it's like looking at a wrinkle-o-meter:

Top shelf: 'The first signs of ageing' - creams for skin just starting to think about throwing in the odd wrinkle

Second shelf: 'With fine lines and wrinkles' - creams for skin becoming a bit more determined

Third shelf: 'With deep lines and wrinkles' - creams for skin starting to win the battle

Bottom shelf (MY shelf): 'More mature skin' - creams for skin that hasn't just said "Hello!" to the wrinkles, but "Hello, can I offer you the comfiest chair in the house and would you like a cuppa?"

Now…the issue with storing products at floor level, is how to get down to them.

Are you a bender or a squatter?

The Squatter: you need good knees (best to warm up before starting this manoeuvre), not be desperate for a wee (once you squat, it's game over), remember to keep your knees together (to avoid a flashing incident) and the ability to balance on your toes – while holding a pot of cream. This leaves only one hand free to steady yourself...when you start to fall over.

The Bender: you need to be flexible (preferably able to touch your toes), not wear a short skirt (to avoid a flashing incident), not get a blood-rush to your head (causing you to topple over into the shelves) and be ready for your bag to swing round from your shoulder, smash itself into you and knock the pot of cream out of your hand.

Creams for us 'mature' ladies should be on the TOP shelf. Let the younger women (who still have the upper hand over their skin) take up a yoga stance to reach down to the floor level shelf. I'm sure THEY won't feel dizzy, have a hot flush and sway slightly when they stand up straight again!

They're Not Dry…They're NOT DRY!

Recognise this little scenario?

You're going on a night out. You intended to take plenty of time getting ready, but instead you've spent far too long down the rabbit hole known affectionately as Facebook. In my case looking at cute videos of dogs, comedians' sketches and friends' posts. I also tend to get trapped in a hell of reading (with disbelief) all the twaddle about losing your meno belly, making your frizzy hair go glossy and suddenly becoming so flexible you're able to do a bridge, a forward roll and the feckin' splits!

I digress...

Suddenly you clock the time and it's a last-minute dash: shower, hair, get dressed and make-up. Preferably in that order. This invariably means that the lovely nail varnish, that matches your outfit perfectly, is on a knife edge as to whether or not it's going to be used.

You're finally ready and desperate to use the little bottle of gorgeousness (your nails for once haven't all broken, and actually look half decent), glancing furtively between the colourful bottle and the clock.

Have you got time? Have you buggery.

Does this stop you? No, it does not.

It's three minutes to the taxi arriving. So, no...you have NOT GOT TIME!

But when has common sense ever got in the way of your desires. Rarely. So, you sit down and quickly apply the varnish. Even deploying the hairdryer to speed up the drying process. Did you have the foresight to pack your handbag, fasten your boots and put your coat on first? Nope...

"Are you ready?! The taxi's nearly here!" shouts your irritated other half up the stairs.

"Alright, alright...I'm coming!" You reply agitatedly. Because you KNOW your nails won't be dry...

So, you hold your hands out in front of you - with the fingers spread-eagled, and try to pick up your handbag and coat using just the tips of your fingers - while panicking about getting any varnish on said handbag and coat because it's fricking impossible to get off!

You then waddle down the stairs, as quickly as you can with your unfastened boots flapping around your ankles, shouting, "Help me put my coat on...shove everything into my handbag...fasten my boots...FFS I need a wee!!

Help me take my coat back off again...open the toilet door...Quick...help me pull my tights and knickers down...hang around to pull them back up again...and open the effin door!

I can't do anything MY NAILS ARE WET!"

This is me...EVERY. SINGLE. TIME.

Dragging My Face Down...

I went mad the other week and bought a pack of those weirdly shaped, fancy foundation sponge applicators. I did this because I'd read that using my fingers to apply my foundation was dragging my face down.

Really!

I have to say...as a sensory, squidgy thing to play with they're lovely. All bouncy and smooth. But as a tool for applying foundation? They're absolutely crap!

First of all, they seem to completely soak up the foundation - just leaving you with a brown sponge that will never be clean again.

Secondly...SECONDLY you have to press them so hard onto your face, to get them to give up any of the foundation they've secreted away, I'm amazed my face hasn't actually been DRAGGED DOWN TO MY KNEES!!
I'm sticking with my fingers, ladies.

*EDIT: apparently, you're meant to wet the sponge first hahahahahahaha!

Flip That Lid!

Do you wear your glasses in the shower?

No? Neither do I…

I took my new brand of shampoo and conditioner into the shower two days ago and couldn't for the life of me get the lid flips to actually…flip. Ages I spent trying to press them down to allow me access to the liquid within. In the end I gave up and unscrewed the bastard lids!

Today I went into the shower and remembered the lid debacle. As hubby was in the bathroom at the same time, I stepped back out of the shower and showed him the bottles - bemoaning the ridiculousness of them not allowing me access to their contents.

He looked at me, and with every fibre of his being tried really hard not to laugh…

Turns out I hadn't removed the plastic seals from the lids…buggery bollox!

Oh Dear…

Just accidentally showered myself with hair conditioner, instead of shower gel.

So at least the pubes I have left will be smooth, shiny, and tangle free!!
Not so happy about the fact that conditioner adds moisture…think there's quite enough of that in my knickers already!!!

Rogue Eyebrows

I reckon my eyebrows need a book of their own. I mean not my real eyebrows…they left the building a long time ago. But my drawn-on eyebrows, which seem to have taken on a persona that is becoming somewhat perturbing!

Need to look permanently surprised?

We got you.

Need to fill the gap between your eyes and your fringe?

We got you.

Need to be saying, 'Hello my friend," with one and "WTF are you talking about?!" with the other?

We got you.

The midlife woman's attempts at drawing on eyebrows leaves a lot to be desired…

Please Can I Have A…

I was on the bus today, and out of the window I spotted an aesthetics shop.

Aesthetics shop!

What's that do you reckon?

Can I go in and choose a new pair of eyebrows, a slimmer arse, a fuller fringe, or nicely toned underarms to replace the crepe bingo wings I currently have?

Can I trade in my saggy jawline for an updated firmer model? Can I return the moustache and beard that I no longer want and didn't actually order in the first place?

On a big sign in their window, they were advertising FAT FREEZING.

WTAF is that all about?!

Are they actually an undercover Iceland for the menopausal woman? Can I lift the lid on one of their many chest freezers and choose a carton of frozen fat? And why would I want a carton of frozen fat?! Is the nation expecting a sudden shortage of lard? Is there a glut of motorbikes that need their cam shafts greasing and only the fat collected from a menopausal woman will be up to the job?

Are they offering to freeze MY fat? Just in case I suddenly lose a lot of weight, miss my blubber and decide I want it back? Or to donate to slimmer ladies who've heard so much about muffin tops they've decided they'd like to give one a go - on a 28-day free return guarantee obviously. You know...for when they realise the error of their ways.

So many questions, so many confused expressions, so many head swivels as the bus trundled on past.

And all of them mine!

PAINTED TOENAILS
Anyone else put their sandals on, realise that nail polish is required then just paint the three visible toes?

WAXING
The Brazilian
For the young and trendy
The Hollywood
For the brave and uninhibited
The Wasteland
For the menopausal woman, no wax required

DRESSED TO IMPRESS…OR NOT

Peepo!

Who in their right mind thinks women want to wear dresses with holes cut out of the sides?

Which nincompoop, in the name of all things holy, thinks this monstrous idea is a go-er?!

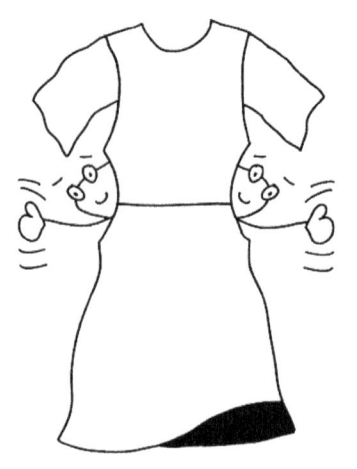

Unbelievably the holes are placed at exactly the right place to showcase our muffin tops. They couldn't have placed them better if they'd tried! Oh, hang on...they did try...and they SUCCEEDED!

Is it so said muffin tops can wink at each other as we walk down the street?

"Well, hello! My owner keeps trying to get rid of me!"

"Mine too! I'm not going anywhere hahahahahaha!"

Is it because someone decided that our midriffs need ventilation and with these natty holes they can now hang out of our dresses, like an excited dog with its head out of a car window?

Is it so our spare tyres can finally take centre stage and enjoy some attention, after being hidden away from public view for so long?

Should we paint googly eyes onto our bulges so it looks like we've got a strange alien hitching a ride on our midriffs; leering out of our dresses and scaring small children and cats?

Brings a whole new meaning to the phrase, 'Hello Boys!' Not sure that ad would've worked quite so well for Eva if she'd been seductively pushing her sides up and out, instead of her boobs.

Clearly someone has lost the plot. Well, they'd better find it again quickly, because the shops are absolutely full of these horrors!

But Yes, I Love the High Heels that I Bought!

My wardrobe, girls, is full of all my lovely tottering heels
I love to strut around in them and still see their appeal.
I struggle now I'm older though
My body's lost its youthful glow,
Let's look at all the issues they reveal…

I walk as if I've wet myself, or like I've come by horse
I take my steps so carefully to try and stay on course.
I clench my toes to hold my shoes
For fear one day a shoe I'll lose,
And sling-backs make the situation worse!

The floor becomes an obstacle, an actual battleground
With smooth and slippy just as bad as rough and harsh, I've found.
The worst by far is bumpy cobbles
Sure to cause the teetering wobbles,
Each tiny stone becomes a hellish mound!

And what about the ground that's soft, let's talk about the grass
I have to walk on tiptoes, oh the woes of being a lass.
I know that if I lower down
I'll end up walking like a clown,
My heels will sink and land me on my ass!

Pavements with their cracks and gaps have simply no respect,
They lie in wait to grab my heels - a trap I now expect.
My heel slips down and with a jolt
My journey comes straight to a halt,
I wrench it out but it's completely wrecked!

High heels are meant to make me walk like sexy movie stars,
When slinking into nightclubs, pubs and bistros, clubs and bars.
They're meant to give me swivelling hips
At least until they make me trip,
Then down I go once more upon my arse!

And then there are the silly straps that some shoes seem to sport,
My foot now flaps, my ankle's loose - there's simply no support.
There's nothing there to firmly grip
I know my feet will surely slip,
But yes, I love the high heels that I bought!

Cheryl and Sandra

Went shopping for a new dress. On the downside I tried on 10 and looked/felt awful in all of them. On the upside I had a lovely chat with two ladies I met in the changing rooms, in a shop aimed at the 'younger woman'.

I could hear them through the curtains trying clothes on, then coming out and showing each other, honestly critiquing their outfits and generally being very kind and supportive.

I was grinning inside my cubicle as I critiqued my own outfits:

"That looks like I could pitch it in the garden and hold a festival in it!"

"Hello world, here's my stomach!"

"Where are these bits meant to go, how the hell does it fasten, why is it like the effin Krypton Factor?!" And most worryingly, "What are the chances of me getting it off?!"

The debate about outfits, across the aisle, continued and I just had to step out and join in. I was met by two very stylish older ladies with fantastic dress sense, and an affection for each other that was clearly obvious. We got chatting - as only women can - and it turned out they were both in their 70s. They'd been friends for 50 years and had supported each other through life's ups and downs.

I applauded all three of us for shopping in this particular shop, and not where society probably felt we should be shopping.

I loved these two ladies for their outlook on life - age is just a number, and we'll dress how we want.

I adored their dress sense & style: one in a white maxi dress accessorised with a wide leather belt; the other in a striped long jumper over bright green jeggings, paired with white pumps.

I wanted to hug them both for flying the flag for older women and breaking society's stereotypes of how older women should look.

We chatted for a while, as if we'd known each other for ages, and when they told me I looked in my mid 40s I told them they were my new best friends.

I asked if I could write about them, after I showed them my Facebook page, and they readily agreed. So, Cheryl and Sandra, if you read this you know who you are. It was a pleasure meeting you, you both put a smile on my face and I don't believe you're in your 70s.

You both looked absolutely fabulous.

May I Present to You, My Belly!

What's going on with this trend of having your shirt half tucked in and half hanging out? What. Is. That. All. About?

My mum would not have let me leave the house dressed like that. She'd have pulled me back to tuck me in properly - shoving the shirt so far down inside my trousers that it reached my knees. Then she'd have hoiked the waistband so far up it would practically be under my armpits...having given me a labia lift en route! At the same time as doing this she'd be admonishing me, telling me that at my age I should've learnt how to dress myself properly.

It just looks like you got dressed in a rush, tucked yourself half in, ran out of time then rushed out of the door to sprint for a bus!

I've just watched a Facebook video of a woman showing me how to do just this, and it had thousands of views.

What in the world?

Apart from anything else, if you're our age with a menopausal belly, why would you tuck the front IN and leave the back OUT? You're basically shouting, "Hello everyone! May I present to you, my belly! It's called Gerald and has had enough of being dressed stylishly (and discreetly covered up) and now wants to take centre stage, be out and proud and is currently discussing terms with its agent for writing its own social media page!"

An Ode to the Maxi Dress

Oh maxi dress, oh maxi dress
My favourite style by far.
I wear it all the time you know
In restaurant, shop and bar.

It covers all the things I've got
I'd rather not be seen.
I'll give a few examples
So you'll know just what I mean.

Pale, white legs that never brown
No matter what I do.
Veins that creep around my shins
A lovely shade of blue.

Hairs so long they'd look ok
On any man I know.
A bum that lost its pertness
And its firmness long ago.

Knees no longer pointing straight
But slipping to the side.
A muffin top and rolls of flab
Are what I'm trying to hide.

I put it on, I stand up tall
And watch it drape around.
All the things kept underneath
Are hidden safe and sound.

So, thank you, lovely maxi dress
For all the times you're there.
Even when you're out of date
It's you I'll always wear.

Rogue Nippleage

Oh. My. Days.

I've just seen that a certain reality 'star' has brought out a faux nipple bra.

Yes…you read that right.

After all these years of trying to cover up rogue nippleage, we are now being encouraged to buy a bra that has false nipples STUCK ON TO THE OUTSIDE of each cup.

FML…

Well, at least if you come across someone wearing one of these horror stories, you'll have somewhere to hang your hat, an implement to clean out your ears with and with a bit of luck - and a quick twiddle - finally be able to pick up alien life in outer space!

Control Pants – My Arse!

If I see one more advert for 'control pants' being modelled on size 8 young women, I am seriously going to lose my twatting temper!

The only control you need in the knicker department at that age is fighting the urge to whip them off and enjoy your still full-on sex drive with your partner, spouse or the person you've been eyeing up at the bus stop for the last two weeks!

At our age, and size, we need to see if these pants WILL actually control anything. Just giving our bellies a stern talking to isn't going to cut it. They need to be well and truly chastised, told they've let everyone down and sent to sit on the naughty step…

Firmly inside our knickers!

Not left hanging out over the top, like a treacherous Judas waiting to present itself to the world the minute we put our clothes on!!

How Long is Your Body?!

What on earth is going on with waistlines on dresses?!

Why are they at least 3" above my actual waist?! With a tie belt that then goes into desperate battle with the incorrectly placed belt loops, as it naturally gravitates to the right place - on my ACTUAL waist - and ends up hanging ridiculously below the dress waistline.

Am I an unusual shape? Other than being menopausally flabby…no!

Is my actual waist alarmingly low? I haven't noticed it dragging along the floor.

Do I have an extremely looooooong body? I'm pretty sure everything is in proportion.

Am I abnormally tall for a woman? Not unless all the other women have suddenly shrunk, and being 5' 5" has made me a giant amongst my kind.

Who is making dresses for incorrectly put together women?!

We're not men…we DO have a waist. Our body goes in, to give dressmakers a clue as to where it is… and it's NOT where they're currently putting it in dresses!

I have so many dresses like this. I've even resorted to safety pinning the tie belt onto the dress waistline, just so it doesn't look so ridiculous when it makes a gallant bid to hang around my actual waist!

Let's Talk About Tights

When putting on tights, are you a sitter or a stander?

Here's what I do:

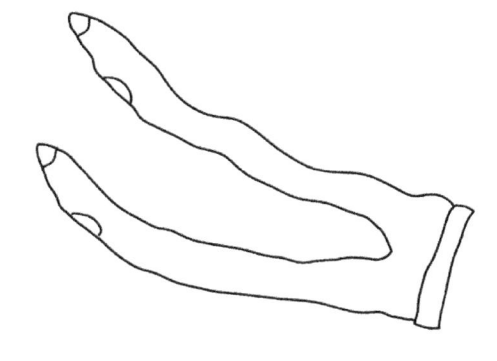

Pull the right leg up first. Practically all the way up - though obviously stopping short of ramming my elbow up my fandango. And then - bizarrely - I roll it back down to my knee again! This allows me to then gather up the left leg. Why didn't I just leave the right one hanging around while we collected its mate in the first place?!

I then stand on my right leg as I hoik the left tight up to my knee, with the desperation of rescuing a drowning man. Feck knows why I stand on one leg; I wonder this every time I do it - as I stagger around the room bouncing against the bed, the door, the wardrobe and sometimes the cat - while desperately doing battle with the wilful nylon.

Once it's up, and my equilibrium is restored, I point my left toe onto the ground (memories of the dim and distant past when I used to do ballet, and in my head I still can) and hoik the left tight all the way up - while simultaneously bending my left leg up into the air. This is akin to the action required for dismounting a horse, looks equally farcical and is often accompanied by a loud fart. My right tight is watching this ludicrous behaviour, while happily loitering around my right knee, comfortable in the knowledge that it won't be joining in.

"Come to mummy, my precious, for your turn is next!"

I now have both legs in my tights and they are nestling happily under my arse. I can practically hear them sighing, 'Thank God for that, our work here is done.' They're wrong. I then stand with legs akimbo and try to convince the waistband to get up over my belly - bit by bit, left side, right side - until eventually I win and my tights take up residence in their final resting place; destined to spend the entire day cutting my body in half.

I'm already counting down the hours until I can rip the buggers off again!

The Scientists Have Been Busy

Saw an advert in a magazine the other day. Apparently, I have a hang-up about my stomach - but I'm not to worry. This company has been working hard on developing innovative technology to make me look like Cindy Crawford in my bathing costume – PHEW!

So, how does this innovative tummy slimming technology work I hear you ask…

Well, here are my suggestions:

1) You drag your bathing costume up your body – tucking your flab in as you go – and an activated voice tells you to take it off again immediately and replace it with a bin bag to completely cover you up.

2) The flab is re-distributed. If my stomach flab is sucked in it can only go to one of two places: under my boobs or around my arse. If it joined forces WITH my boobs I'd be over the moon – for the first time in my life I'd actually have a decent pair of boobs! But UNDER my boobs…not so much. If it settled around my arse that wouldn't be good either. Kim Kardashian might have a humungous arse, but it's still pert…if mine became humungous it'd just look like a sack of spuds arguing about needing more space.

3) The swimming costume is actually made of well disguised industrial metal and is able to successfully contain the population of a small Caribbean Island; so, dealing with my stomach flab won't be an issue. Only problem is I'll not

be able to breathe, and will most likely feel sick – plus my ability to drink a shed load of cocktails by the pool will be seriously diminished.

4) The swimming costume is magic, and the minute it comes into contact with my stomach several inches of flab instantly disappear.

The thing is ladies…I'm just glad to know that innovative technology is being put to such good use. It's great to know that our stomach flab is keeping technologists and/or scientists awake at night!

The Sandal Scandal

It's summer again…sandal shopping time. This fills me with dread every bloody year.

It's not that I'm fussy but I have quite odd feet.

I can't do 'completely flat' because of knackered arches from years of doing ballet and I end up with plantar fasciitis - ouch.

I can't do 'barely there strappy' because my feet are long and knobbly and would look more at home on a hobbit.

I can't do 'ankle straps' because they don't hold my feet in place and end up flopping off the sides, plus my heels don't make for pleasant viewing.

I can't do 'sling backs' because the sling backs sling off and I end up walking out of them.

I can't do 'flip-flops' because the toe thong tickles too much – I have a very low tickle threshold.

I can't do 'kitten heels' because I seem to have to clench my toes to keep them on - the sandals not my toes.

I can't do 'thin strap across the toes' because my toes look like a deranged set of piano keys that a camel would be proud of.

Add into the mix the fact that I don't want a pair that say 'safe, comfy, middle-aged' or a pair that say 'stripper' and you can only begin to imagine the trauma that is sandal shopping for me. I tend to hang onto pairs that are comfy and wear them for years.

But sometime, just sometimes, I fancy a new up-to-date pair.

It Shouldn't Be This Difficult!

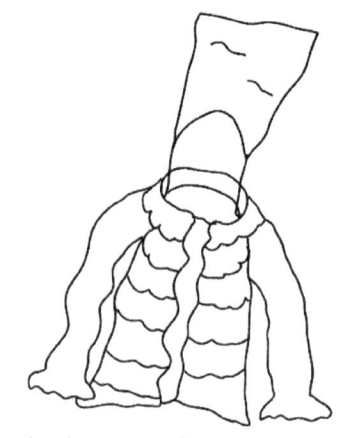

Which sadist came up with the idea of attaching a vest top to the inside of a floaty, frilly blouse?!

One morning I decided to wear one of said blouses to work. FML! Trying to peer into its insides I longingly searched for the sleeve straps of the vest top bit. I located them eventually, then wondered how to get my arms through both them AND the floaty sleeves of the blouse.

At the same time.

How do you hold the vest top straps open while negotiating the floaty sleeves - in tandem?

I decided to just dive in and hope for the best. First mistake. I ended up trying to force my head through one of the vest top straps. I quickly retrieved it, before completely cutting off my air supply, and decided to try again. Surely it can't be that difficult?! Second mistake.

I dived in again and managed to coordinate my left arm into both the left-hand vest top strap AND the left-hand blouse sleeve - at the same time. Get me! I then ventured towards the right-hand set of sleeves and really went for it. I shoved my head in via the bottom of the blouse, hoping it would successfully navigate its way to the two neck holes of the attached tops, and burst through into the fresh air triumphantly. But this was not to be. And I couldn't even SEE the right-hand set of sleeves!

Turned out I'd somehow managed to get my left arm in BOTH vest top straps - both I tell you! I was now flailing around in a sea of chiffon, which had an ever-tightening grip on me. I thought I was going to have to shout for hubby to come and rescue me, by possibly cutting me out of the damn thing!

In the end I managed to remove my head (not literally), and pull my arm out of possibly THREE sleeves. I then swore loudly and threw the top into a corner.

A simple jumper had never looked quite so inviting...

Big Knickers, or Instruments of Torture?

I've decided that I'll no longer be wearing my big squeeze it all in/tummy control/spandex knickers. Call them what you like; instruments of torture, is my preferred term.

Big 'squeeze-it-all-in' knickers are great in theory but in reality, I ask you, where does all the fat actually go?

It would be great to think it was going to be pushed up into my bra to give me a decent pair of boobs, but alas no.

It actually does two things – neither of which is the slightest bit helpful.

The fat squeezed up and out of the top settles in a roll just below my bra, making me look like Hattie Jacques in *Carry on Matron*. The fat squeezed down and out of the bottom settles in a roll across my thighs, making me look like a Russian shot putter that's gone to seed.

The overall look is a doughnut with an elastic band round its middle. And we're not talking a fresh pink icing covered, sprinkle topped, jam filled doughnut. Oh no... this is a left out in the sun, sweaty, icing covered, mould-topped, angst-filled menopausal doughnut - with the odd white, wiry hair sticking out in random places!

And don't you just love them in the heat!

You come back to the house, peel them off your arse, coax them out of places they shouldn't even have considered venturing to and have to practically wring them out!

Suddenly the dreaded cheese cutter style sounds tempting...

And another thing, my body seems to have made a rather distressing development where said big knickers are concerned.

If I bend over - while wearing tracksuit bottoms - my stomach flab flops over the top of my knickers and starts to roll them down.

This is very depressing in the house. It's EXTREMELY ALARMING in the supermarket!

Choose Your Knickers Wisely…

Let's talk about our knickers girls
I really think we should.
We'll cover all the different types:
The ugly, bad and good.

We'll start with silly scraps of lace,
That look more like a doily.
The sort that's meant to tantalise,
When taken off so slowly.
You know the ones; they itch like mad –
All frilly bits and bows.
Leave them where they'll do less harm -
In shops, arranged in rows.

And while we're in the area,
Of underwear that's wrong,
The next offender, please step up –
The bloody awful thong!
I feel our bum cheeks need to be
Contained and wrapped up tight.
Not there to see through trousers,
Bumps and lumps and cellulite!

And as for silly G-Strings,
Someone tell me, what the hell?
A bit of string rammed up your bum?
That surely won't end well!
French knickers, what's that all about?
They're meant to look all naughty.

But we all know that actually,
They're flappy, loose and draughty!

Hipster and bikini briefs -
Now this type makes me frown.
They sit below your stomach,
And your flab then rolls them down!
High cut briefs cause fat to sit,
Below your knicker line.
No wonder that we've had to turn
To vodka, gin and wine!

So, what about 'control' dear friends -
The 'suck it all in' knicker.
Designed to make our tum look thin,
Yet other bits look thicker!
These pants are like elastic bands,
They pull it all in tight.
But where does all that fat end up?
It's not a pretty sight

Basically, the fat is pushed
Above the straining band.
You end up with an extra roll;
Your under rib expands.
Don't try to eat, don't try to drink,
Don't even try to sit.
In fact you're best not trying to move,
In case your knickers split!

Trying to get them on is the
Olympics at their best.

A medal would be well deserved,
For simply getting dressed.
And don't begin to *ever* think,
You'll get them off no worry.
You need a wee? There's just no way,
They'll come off in a hurry.

Well girls, what's left for us to wear;
Which knickers should we buy?
My favourite is the full cut brief,
It's classic and here's why.

The waist band comes up all the way,
Above your flab and fat.
They don't make claims to change your shape,
Or squash your stomach flat.
They let you breathe; they don't roll down,
Or cut your bum in two.
They do not itch, or flap around;
They're solid through and through.

So what's the style that's right for you?
I ponder on your views.
Make sure they're comfy, do the job -
Whichever ones you choose.

How Long is this Feckin Belt?!

Just had a successful girls' shopping and boozy lunch day.

Everything was going swimmingly until I decided to try on a crossover, wraparound dress. Any dress that requires a degree in mechanical engineering should be avoided at all costs. I can never work out how to get into the damn thing, or which bit goes where. Especially when it comes with a 10' long belt that apparently has to go round your body three times and between your legs twice, before it eventually pops out through a slit in the side to create a huge bow with its mate.

Straight off I couldn't fasten the secret inside button - my stomach was unhelpfully refusing to move out of the way to allow me to see what I was doing. When I'd finally managed to get both parts of the dress fastened the front was gaping open and my boobs were hanging out. And then when I decided I didn't actually like it I couldn't get the chuffing thing off!

My arms were trapped upwards, my head was poking out of the front and my stomach had declared all-out war on the panel secured by the bastard secret inside button - which I now couldn't bloody unfasten!

When I'd eventually managed to extricate myself from this instrument of torture (masquerading as a clothing garment) the static in the fabric had caused my hair to stand on end, I'd had a monumental hot flush, an uncontrollable sneezing fit and thanked the menopausal Gods that I'd had my pee pad in place!

Mucho wino was drunk at lunch...

You Didn't Want to Use the Loo Did You?

The jumpsuit - clearly created by a man who has never actually EVER worn one! For the love of God, why?!

Don't get me wrong; a jumpsuit can look lovely. Except on me. On me I end up looking like I've got arrows coming at me from every direction, pointing to my now highlighted stomach. It feels like I'm wearing a sign around my neck shouting, "Roll up! Roll up! Here's my meno belly!" I've seen them looking gorgeous on other women - just not on me.

What I'm complaining about though, is the practicality of it. Or to be more precise, the struggle of going to the toilet while wearing one.

Here are my issues:

1) The WHOLE THING has to come down. So, do you:

- let your entire outfit pool on the floor around your feet

OR

- worry about the state of the toilet floor and quickly try to scoop it up before it hits the ground - while taking it down at the SAME TIME...

2) Once you've got it down, you're left sitting on the loo naked apart from your bra, with your stomach now happily resting on your knees.

3) To put it back on you have to stand up from the loo while SIMULTANEOUSLY scooping the jumpsuit up. This means you have a bunched up, scrunched up outfit in your hands which you then have to ease back up to your shoulders, while STILL trying to prevent it from hitting the manky floor.

God help you if you need the toilet quickly! There is NO WAY IN HELL that bitch of an outfit is going to allow you to go to the loo at the last minute. And if you're drunk, rush to the loo and attempt to take your 'trousers' down while forgetting they're attached to your top...well...that's a whole other scenario.

Anyone ever done this? *asking for a friend...

Plan your toilet trips well ahead ladies...plan them well ahead.

What's That on Your Head?!

Some people put on a woolly hat and are instantly transported into a snow filled, jingle-belled romantic comedy. You know the kind…where the leading man and woman spend the entire film hating each other, then at the end it snows. She puts on the magic woolly hat and looks divine; her pink cold nose is cuteness personified and - as the snowflakes land on their eyelashes - they fall head over heels in love. The end.

I on the other hand, look like I've been let out on day-release, with a runny nose, pouring eyes, flattened hair desperately trying to make a bid for freedom and a head that looks like it's been rammed into a furry condom!!!

Has it Gone Yet?

Just watched a video telling me what kind of dress to wear to hide my 'meno belly'.

Naturally I was all ears! What kind of magic dress is about to be presented to me, I wondered.

I should've been suspicious when I clocked that the woman modelling it was no older than 30...with no twatting belly in sight!

Basically, it's a dress with frills on the hem and frills on the sleeves...to DISTRACT people's eyes away from my belly oh...and an elasticated waist that sits perfectly ABOVE my belly! Oh, how I laughed! For a start any waistline that sits above your belly is basically shouting to anyone who'll listen "BEHOLD! CHECK OUT MY FECKIN' BELLY!"

And if I wanted to distract people's eyes away from my belly, I'm not convinced that a few frills are up to the job. How about I don fishnets and employ my jazz hands in front of these people? Or skip into a room backwards singing the *National Anthem*? Or, as a piece de resistance paint my face like a clown, add a plastic red nose and enter the room in a full-blown clown car while balancing a bucket of water on my head!

If I did any of these things people would be so busy trying to escape me, my 'meno belly' would be the furthest thing from their mind...never mind their effin eyes!

What on Earth?

I've just been for a mooch around one of my favourite massive, high-street shops…Bugger me backwards and call me Susan - what on earth have they done to the sizings?!

Instead of the usual 8, 10, 12, 14 etc it's now S, M, L, XL etc. WTF! Do I look like a coffee, a bag of pasta or a glass of wine?! I could do with the latter right now, I can tell you!

I searched the label for a clue as to which size I was: nothing, nada, zilch. I even dug around in the bottom of my bag for my reading glasses so I could double check!

I found a very helpful assistant who was as pissed off as me about this new set-up and she explained:

S = 8-10
M = 12-14
L = 16-18

Err…what's happened to size 14-16??

I am beyond incensed at this ridiculousness.

Are retailers just trying to make our life as a woman as difficult as possible? It was bad enough knowing that a size 14 is NOT the same in different styles, different garments and different shops…but now we have to battle our way through different shops' interpretation of S, M, L, XL etc!

I was so cross I had to go to a coffee shop and have a S bag of crisps, an M sandwich, an L latte and a feckin XL cake!!

Ankle Boots of the Devil

Found these lovely ankle boots. That's the last time the word 'lovely' will be used in the same sentence as these boots.

No form of opening to allow you to get the chuffers on, what-so-ever! Just a little loop at the back. That's the only form of assistance you're going to get.

So…always up for a challenge I decided I would not be defeated by a buggering boot. I put my foot in - vertically you understand - then started to squeeze it down into the depths of the unknown. I tried jiggling and stamping, but the boot was point-blank refusing me an audience with its mysterious innards. Obviously, I couldn't do it unaided so masterly I deployed the little loop.

Masterly my arse!

Now remember, I'd been standing with all my weight on one leg for a bit and there was only so long I could hold the balance. Well, not for very long at all as it turned out.

As I bent down to pull the loop - and hopefully finally get the bastard boot on - my shoulder bag swung round and bashed me on my raised foot: I jolted with surprise, completely lost my balance and toppled forward into the unsuspecting shelves! Luckily, they'd been attached to the wall as a permanent fixture and not just placed there as a free-standing unit that was merely passing by.

The boot had obviously sent out a distress signal and its mates had dutifully thrown themselves off the shelves to give the bonkers woman with the crazy hair and mad eyes a severe talking to! An assistant had to come and help clear away the carnage I'd surrounded myself with.

"Sorry, sorry I'm menopausal and have lost all sense of balance, dignity and knowledge of my ability in the trying-on-of-boots department."

I DID NOT buy the boots as I feel I have enough trouble in the day trying to get my knickers on without falling over…so I don't particularly want my footwear to launch an all-out attack on my personage as well!

Harrummmph!

I went clothes shopping, because I had some birthday money to spend…why can you never find anything to buy when you actually have some flipping dosh?

I tried on a long blouse to go over my trusty leggings, but for some reason the designer had decided that 'long blouse' also meant 'arms of an orangutan'. I just knew the sleeves were going to end up being dragged through the butter, the spaghetti bolognese and the hummus.

I then went onto a jumpsuit, with a wide waist scarf that fastened at the front. 'Marvellous,' I thought, this will hide my belly. Wrong…my belly appeared below the wide scarf. And the print had white flowers with black centres. Two of which rested ON my belly, so from the side it looked like it was winking at me. 'Feck that for a game of soldiers,' I thought to myself, 'Don't really want a sarcastic belly, thanks very much!'

Next up, a lime green dress. This shade of green is my absolute favourite colour, which stems from my love of lime cream soda pop as a child. Now I drool over everything lime coloured and lime flavoured.

I'm weird.

This dress had a side zip, to create a large hole down one side. When trying to get it on I took a wrong turn and triumphantly popped my head up out of this helpful hole. Helpful hole, my arse! As I stared down at the sleeves I was confused, I didn't remember this dress having a trouser attachment. Having realised my mistake I extricated my head, rather like coming out of a birth canal, put it through the correct hole and pulled the dress down into place. Glancing in the mirror, in the hope of seeing perfection, I was instead met by disappointment.

The ruched front, which I'd had high hopes for, instead of hiding my belly actually accentuated it. And then I tried to get it off and the helpful side hole, not content with only a bit part in this debacle, decided to provide an encore.

Lastly was a lovely chiffon top. All I have to say about this is that the chiffon was so sheer I looked like I was coyly trying to sell my wares behind a cheap lace curtain.

I left the cubicle, harrumphed my way out of the shop and went straight to a cafe to console myself with sweet treats; because obviously that's going to help me look good in dresses…

Pick Me! Pick Me!

Who else has different categories of clothes?

- for going 'out, out' (recline in the wardrobe in all their barely worn glory thinking they're the kingpins, the dog's bollox and numero uno)

- for going 'out' (worn whenever leaving the house is required, about to complain to their union rep for overwork and under-appreciation)

- for going to work (desperately want to be in the other two categories, but we're not wearing those bad boys anywhere other than a place of employment)

- for the Summer (I say Summer, I mean that one day in the U.K. when the sun comes out, it stops raining and every BBQ in the land is hurriedly lit. At this point our flimsy dresses, short skirts and vest tops will fight to the death to be the one outfit chosen for such a momentous occasion)

- for Winter (we often attempt to move these items somewhere else in the months of June, July and August, but really, why bother? These guys are what we know the best, as they spend most of the year adorning our bodies)

- PYJAMAS (♪♫ CE-LE-BRATE GOOD TIMES, COME ON! ♪♫ do, do, do, doo, do, do, do, dooo)

Stand By Belt Loops – Your Time Has Come!

I've just watched a video of a young woman with a stomach so flat it would give an ironing board a run for its money, telling me how to dress to hide my BELLY!

Showing me how to tuck my top in to my BELT LOOP! Cos that's really going to make my traitorous midriff disappear! It's my fat I need tucking in somewhere love, not a corner of my buggering top!

For the love of all things holy…stop showing me how to hide things you don't even have!

Otherwise, I'll start making videos showing people how to hide a Porsche, a butler, a 50-foot yacht and a twatting hair free chin!

STREWTH!

A Glutton for Punishment

Note to self…DO NOT TRY CLOTHES ON IN SHOPS WEARING A FRIGGIN JUMPER!

I did this the other day. What on earth was I thinking…

At one point I nearly yelled at the top of my voice, "I'm so effin hot in here, someone hose me down NOW!"

In one particular shop (just to spice things up further) a long thin mirror behind me was angled off the wall. Every time I bent down to pull trousers or a skirt up, I banged into it and heard it ricochet off the wall and wobble on its fixings. At one point I'm sure it whispered, "That's what you get for having such a fat arse…"

I thought it was just me, but there was a constant percussion section provided by all the other ladies behind their cubicle curtains doing the exact same thing – accompanied by an exasperated chorus of WTF?!

Anyhoo…I came away empty handed apart from a sweaty back courtesy of my jumper, a red mark on my nose because I forgot to remove my specs before pulling a top with a tight neck hole down over my face, a head full of static hair - what is that all about?! - and a bruise on my arse from the bastard mirror!

Oh. My. Days…

Just been for a wee.
Wearing my long cardi.
The long cardi has a very long belt.
The belt was undone.

And hanging down behind me.
Unnoticed.

I'll leave the rest of this very short story to your imagination….

Ouch! Again…

Lost a battle with my dressing gown this morning.

Got the inside tie accidentally trapped inside my knickers, whipped it off with more vim and vigour than was strictly necessary and seriously thought I was going to be scraping my fanny flaps off the TWATTING WALL!!!!

> ***SQUEAK!***
> I've put my sandals on and they've started to squeak!
> I'm walking around sounding like there are two mice hot on my heels having frantic sex. Either that or my knickers need a good dose of WD40!

TRYING ON A DRESS
Went clothes shopping today.
Only thing I came home with was a pulled muscle from getting stuck in a dress!

NEW BRA
Had my boobs measured for the first time since entering the menopause.
My new bra is holding them up so high, cold ears will never be an issue again!

GOOSEY LOOSEY
Nothing makes you feel old like wearing 3" stilettoes and realising you're waddling around like a drunk goose with incontinence issues…

BIG PANTS
Put on my new big pants today.
They're above my jeans.
Watch out youths – menopausal
women are on trend…

SPORTS BRA
The work of the devil
- need a physics degree to get it on
- need to be double-jointed to get it off

SUMMER DRESS
Your summer dress: If you sit on that plastic chair in the sun, for even five minutes, I'm gonna cling to your arse cheeks like a wet shower curtain, the minute you stand up!

An Ode to The Dressing Gown

Dressing gown, oh dressing gown
You're simply my best mate,
You always fit and wrap around
Regardless of my weight.

You're soft and you are fluffy
You are there no matter what,
You're always here to comfort me
Except for when I'm hot!

Feeling sad and feeling miserable
Or happy, fab and great,
Feeling angry with my body
You will always be my mate.

You never ask for anything
I'll always care for you,
Except for when your belt comes loose
And dangles in the loo.

And sorry for the crumbs I keep
Amongst your fulsome folds,
Also for the threadbare bits
And occasional tiny hole.

So dressing gown don't ever change
Don't take your love away,
Just stay with me throughout my life
You really make my day.

OY! Listen Up!

Clothes shops, please listen
We don't need a label
All we need is nice clothes,
And then we'll be able

To make our own choices
On what we will wear,
And not wait for you
To decide on our fare.

So pack it in please
With your plus sizes naming,
We don't need a 'fat' shop
Or our body size shaming.

Our weight shouldn't matter
Or alter our style,
And just cos we're bigger
We still want to smile.

We want to feel sexy
We want to feel lush,
We don't want short tops
Barely covering our bush!

We want styles that flatter
Our menopause bods,
We don't want a gamble
With all of the odds…

Stacked against us while hoping
Your clothes might just fit.
But fit our WHOLE body
Not flattening our tits!

We haven't become aliens
Because we are ageing,
Our shape is just changing
And YOU leave us raging!

We don't need to hear
Names like plus size or curvy,
And tolerate everything
Black, brown or navy.

We want to wear fashion
And styles that will flatter,
We want to hear, "Ladies
Your size doesn't matter!"

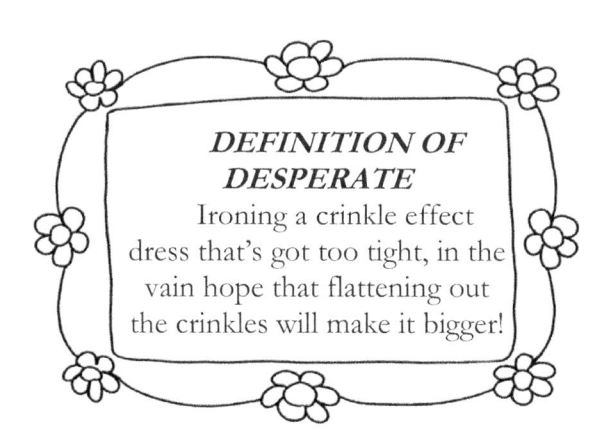

DEFINITION OF DESPERATE
Ironing a crinkle effect dress that's got too tight, in the vain hope that flattening out the crinkles will make it bigger!

HANDBAG

Just driven to the shops with the seatbelt warning sign flashing and peeping at me, because my heavy handbag was on the passenger seat.
I refuse to take handbag advice from a bloody car!

KNICKERS IN A TWIST

Now I realise why today wasn't one of my finest.

I got undressed for bed and discovered I'd been wearing my knickers inside out!

That explains why it felt like my gusset had been trying to exfoliate my fanny all day!

FA, LA, LA, LA, LAAA...

The Girls Are Out on the Town

Here's what happened on our last girls' Christmas night out...

I spent the morning laying everything out:

- dress (long-sleeved to cover up flabby armpits - yes...not just bingo wings, flabby armpits too!)

- shoes (4" red patent leather – I kid you not, there's life in the old gal yet)

- underwear (including support tights and suck-it-all-in knickers)

- handbag (large enough to hold pee pads, reading glasses and earplugs)

- make-up (thick enough to fill in the wrinkles)

- jewellery

I spent the afternoon pacing around waiting to put it all on and decided that 3pm was probably pushing it a bit, so dutifully hung on until 5pm – and even then, I only just managed to be ready for 7pm. God knows what I was doing for two hours! Mind you, the support tights took nearly half an hour to pull on – with a break half way to mop up sweat, swear profusely and lie down from exhaustion.

After a meal in town, and cocktails, followed by a few hours at a cabaret club, we headed for the taxi rank – happy. But as we approached it, one of our number suggested a snifter before heading home.

Oh hello! What a marvellous idea!

We quickly staggered towards a bar, with the most amazing internal décor – designed to look like an old church. Obviously, it wasn't actually an old church – I'm pretty sure there must be laws about turning churches into dens of alcohol, dancing and hot, eager young men.

Did I mention the hot, eager, young men?

We quickly found a booth, sat down then quickly leapt up again. The music was incredible: 80s, 90s and recognisable current stuff – we all screamed unnecessarily loudly when a *Saturday Night Fever* medley was thrown into the mix!

We left at 2.30AM! 2.30AM I TELL YOU!!!

- one of us was grabbed by an aforementioned hot, eager, young man and offered a snog on the way out (obviously she politely declined the offer – while grinning from ear to ear)

- one of us struggled to walk

- one of us struggled to speak

- one of us struggled to see

- one of us got into an altercation at the taxi rank when some young whipper-snappers tried to push in front of us

The young might struggle at times to see, or even acknowledge, us mid-lifers but they can certainly hear us when they piss us off!

Don't cross a group of menopausal women high on life, full of cocktails, dancing in the street to *I Will Survive* and elated at the fact that they've managed to stay awake long enough to be out late.

A truly fantastic night out!

I'm Going In!

Don't you just love the annual 'hunt down a couple of outfits for the party season' debacle. Or as I like to call it – the 'try to find something that doesn't make me look like mutton-dressed-as-lamb, has an air of Liz Hurley about it (as opposed to an air of desperation), and doesn't cost the earth' time of year.

Here's how my last attempt went…

Day 1: I scooped up 14 (14 I tell you!) dresses and dragged them into the changing room. By number 2 I was downhearted, by number 6 I was pissed off, by number 10 I was depressed and by number 14 I wanted to strangle the assistant who asked through the cubicle door, "Is everything alright Madam?"

Day 2: I tried on two more. One turned out to be a short-legged jumpsuit rather than a dress. I only discovered this after trying to get into it for FIVE MINUTES! Wearing the legs as sleeves was interesting. It was also covered in cheap gold sparkle, which I'm still prising out of my hair, and picking out of my teeth to this day. The other dress turned out to be a long top, which would explain my horror at finding splits that went all the way up to my armpits. Not even I would wear that with my usual thick tights and boots combo. I do have limits – just.

Day 3: I tried on a normal length jumpsuit and a black, criss-cross style dress. The dress made me look like a squashed pear trying to burst out of a string bag. I'm not even prepared to discuss the jumpsuit.

Day 4: I picked out 10 more outfits. While trying them on I suddenly realised that my armpits (yes, my actual armpits!) have become very flabby – they've obviously decided to come out in sympathy with my bingo wings. I'd not really noticed them being that bad before, but today they were out and proud. In EVERY. SINGLE. DRESS.

I left the shop in mourning for my taut, flab-free armpits, came home, resorted to the internet and ordered two identical long-sleeved dresses: one black, one red.

Day 5: The dresses arrived. I opened the parcel with trepidation and slowly took them out. I tried the red one on first and turned to the mirror and…wow… it fitted. Not only did it fit, it looked great! I quickly added tights, shoes and jewellery and admired myself. Then immediately took it off again and tried on the black one (I know it's the same dress, but you understand ladies…) I looked fab!

So, two dresses I'm thrilled with: length just above the knee (providing an air of sexiness), nicely shaped (successfully hiding all my lumps and bumps), tastefully lacy and long-sleeved (keeping my flabby armpits and bingo wings well and truly under wraps).

RESULT!

The 12 Days of Midlife

On the first day of midlife my body gave to me – a bumper pack of Tena La-dy (We should get these free on the NHS you know)

On the second day of midlife my body gave to me – 2 painful boobs (Don't hug me, don't touch me, don't come anywhere near me!)

On the third day of midlife my body gave to me – flabby bingo wings (Seriously, it's like bloody jelly)

On the fourth day of midlife my body gave to me – 4 tubes of lube (If you have to ask what it's for, you're not middle-aged yet...)

On the fifth day of midlife my body gave to me – 5…whis…kery….chins (I'm seriously going to have to start shaving)

On the sixth day of midlife my body gave to me – 6 murderous thoughts (Nobody is safe I tell you…NOBODY)

On the seventh day of midlife my body gave to me – blue varicose veins (Yes! And they're ALL on the same leg!)

On the eighth day of midlife my body gave to me – dry frizzy hair (I can't do an effin' thing with it!)

On the ninth day of midlife my body gave to me – a fat wobbly belly (Dear God in heaven – when is that going to go?)

On the tenth day of midlife my body gave to me – 10 sleepless nights (Only 10?! I now make the walking dead look good!)

On the eleventh day of midlife my body gave to me – 11 flaming flushes (Somebody clearly took me seriously when I said I wanted to be 'hot' after 50)

On the twelfth day of midlife my body gave to me…sorry, what was I saying? (Do I know you?)

Oh yes…On the twelfth day of midlife my body gave to me:

12 something or others
11 flaming flushes
10 sleepless nights
A fat wobbly belly
Dry frizzy hair
Blue varicose veins
6 murderous thoughts
5 whis…kery… chins….
4 tubes of lube
Flabby bingo wings
2 painful boobs
and a bumper pack of Tena La-dy!!!

If you didn't sing that I'm very disappointed.

Decs Down, Lolls Out!

Want to know how long it took me to take the decs down last Christmas? Four and a half hours!

Do we live in a mansion? No.

Do we have a tree in every room? No.

Do we have 10,000 fairy lights strewn around the place? No.

Do we have every single room decorated? No.

So, what causes this absurdly slow pace?

Me. I can't be arsed.

I'm always STILL in my pyjamas when I do this job, so each comfy chair I walk past beckons me over for a loll. And a chocolate obvs! I sat down at the dining table for a quick look at Facebook and an hour later I was still there, having got sucked into videos of *Motherland*, *Don't Tell the Bride* and *The Dog House*.

"Just one more," I kept saying to myself, "And this will be the last."

Hahahahahahaha!

"No! Get up and get on with the job" I replied quietly; too quietly it turned out, because I couldn't hear myself. However, I had no problem hearing myself when I then said, 'Ooo, look at that cute dog…I just need to check that this couple adopt it. Maybe I'll pause it, go and make a coffee, open a nice tin of biscuits then move to the sofa to make sure I don't miss the happy ending.'

The dog got adopted.

Phew!

I then walked around in a very lacklustre fashion, feebly wafting a duster in the general direction of the surfaces, while contemplating giving into it and going upstairs for a bloody nap!

EDIT: I abandoned it and went for a soak in a warm bath instead - with a good book and a glass of red!

Cheers…

Merry Fa La La-ing Christmas!

Deck the halls with boughs of holly
Fa la la la la la la la la!
Stressed out mum's not feeling jolly
Fa la la la la la la la la!

Grumpy teens won't put their phones down
Fa la la la la la la la la!
Dad's about to have a meltdown
Fa la la la la la la la la!

Get the cat out of the tree
Fa la la la la la la la la!
Make poor mum a gin - or three
Fa la la la la la la la la!

Aunt Joan's farting like a trooper
Fa la la la la la la la la!
Dad's now in a drunken stupor
Fa la la la la la la la la!

Sprouts are soggy, turkey's chewy
Fa la la la la la la la la!
Gravy's lumpy, mash is gluey
Fa la la la la la la la la!

Carrots welded to the roaster
Fa la la la la la la la la la!
Who shoved parsnips in the toaster?
Fa la la la la la la la la!

Little Timmy's nose is pouring
Fa la la la la la la la la!
Spilt bread sauce has ruined the flooring
Fa la la la la la la la la!

Pigs in blankets burnt and crispy
Fa la la la la la la la la!
Cousin Mabel's found the whiskey
Fa la la la la la la la la!

Christmas pudding's soaked in brandy
Fa la la la la la la la la!
Toddler's sick from eating candy
Fa la la la la la la la la!

Uncle Norman's started swearing
Fa la la la la la la la la!
Can't believe what Aunt Vi's wearing
Fa la la la la la la la la!

She's proclaimed she is a singer
Fa la la la la la la la la!

But she looks more like a swinger
Fa la la la la la la la la!

Grandad's getting drunk and lairy
Fa la la la la la la la la!
Gran's false teeth are on the fairy
Fa la la la la la la la la!

Legs being humped by naughty Rover
Fa la la la la la la la la!
Mum's pretending to be sober
Fa la la la la la la la la!

Look around at all the faces
Fa la la la la la la la la!
Loving kisses and embraces
Fa la la la la la la la la!

Family's what makes Christmas dear
Fa la la la la la la la la!
At SOMEONE ELSE'S please, next year!
FA LA LA LA LAA…. LA LA LA L'AARRGH!!

Ding Dong!

Do you remember when we used to get carol singers turning up on our doorsteps?

I particularly remember one year when a group of teenagers grunted one line of 'We Wish You a Merry Christmas' then knocked on the door, held their hands out for money and just stood staring at me.

I opened the door, took one look at them and said, "Absolutely not! Unless you sing me a WHOLE carol. I'm quite partial to *Silent Night*, for ease I'll accept *Away in a Manger* but if you really want to impress me, you'll attempt *Oh Little Town of Bethlehem* – complete with descant."

Then I shut the door and stood back to listen.

Retreating footsteps is all I heard, ladies…retreating footsteps.

Dear Santa…

Thanks very much for the gin, wine, chocolates and fancy pants biscuits.

However, I don't remember asking for the roll of fat that's now hanging out BELOW my knickers.

WTF?

Please come back and collect it ASAP.

Yours,
Disgruntled of Durham

To Decorate or Not to Decorate

Hubby and I went out for a coffee to a charming little café with a gift shop attached. After finishing our drinks, I obviously went for a wander around the shop.

I instantly spotted, and rushed over to, a display of gorgeous Christmas decorations. Much stroking, admiring and cooing ensued. Hubby quickly appeared by my side and told me – in no uncertain terms – that I DID NOT NEED any more Christmas decorations.

Red. Rag. To. A. Bull…

If I hadn't been considering buying something before – I certainly was now.

I found a stylish snowman (can those two words actually appear in the same sentence?) and bought it - with a raised eyebrow sideways glance at hubby. I then told him that he was quite correct: I didn't NEED more Christmas decorations however, I did WANT them.

I also pointed out that he was lucky I'd gone for the 10-inch wooden snowman instead of the 3-foot tall knitted one. The 4-foot reindeer made out of sticks had also caught my eye, as had the 5-foot twinkling tree AND the massive wreath of dried fruit, seed pods and red painted cinnamon sticks. If we'd had a mantelpiece the 12-foot-long pine cone and holly garland, covered in fake snow, would also have been making its way to the till with me!

All things considered I think he got off lightly…

Oh…
(Based on the song *Let it Snow* written by Sammy Cahn and Jule Styne in 1945)

Oh, the meno is rather frightful
Its symptoms are just delightful.
And now my farts ebb and flow

Let 'em blow, let 'em blow, let 'em blow…

Menopause Is Coming to Town

(Based on the song *Santa Claus is Coming to Town* written by J. Fred Coots and Haven Gillespie in 1934)

You better watch out,
You better not cry
Your hair's falling out
I'm telling you why
Menopause is coming to town

It's making a list
Of all of the crap
That's coming your way
Shove lube up your flap
Menopause is coming to town

It's here to stop you sleeping
And grow a lovely beard
It will dry out your moistened bits
Make you fat just as you feared.

Oh…

You better watch out,
You better not cry
You'll wee when you cough
I'm telling you why
Menopause is coming to town…

Oh Pissmas Tree, Oh Pissmas Tree…

Oh, pissmas tree, oh pissmas tree
I really need a Tena
Oh, pissmas tree, oh pissmas tree
Cos now I'm in the mena
If I should cough, or laugh or sneeze
I have to quickly cross my knees.
Oh, pissmas tree, oh pissmas tree
Cos now I'm in the mena…

Rudolph the Hot-Flush Reindeer

(Based on the song *Rudolph the Red Nosed Reindeer* written by Jonny Marks in 1949)

Rudolph the hot flush reindeer
Had a very shiny nose,
And very hairy outbreaks
Specially on her chin and toes.

All of the other reindeer
Didn't understand her plight,
They thought she'd just got chunky
Now her reindeer coat was tight.

Then one foggy Christmas Eve
Tena came to say,
Rudolph pull your pants up quick
These will keep the wee away.

Now all the other reindeers
Think that Rudolph is the best,

She's found that HRT has
Brought her back her fun and zest!

Frosty the Snowgal
(Based on the song *Frosty the Snowman* written by Walter "Jack" Rollins and Steve Nelson in 1950)

Frosty the snowgal
Was a jolly pissed-off soul,
With a big round tum and a bulging chest
If she fell down she would roll.
Frosty the snowgal
Knew the meno was to blame,
With her buttons made of coal undone
Nothing fitted - oh the shame.

There must've been some magic in
Those suck-it-all-in-knicks,
For when she placed them on her arse
She was slimmer than a stick.

Frosty the snowgal
Thought, 'To squash it is a sin,'
So, she whipped them off, threw them far away
Ate a feast and drank some gin.

Last Christmas
(Based on the song *Last Christmas* written by George Michael in 1984)

Last Christmas I tried not to fart
But the very next day I did anyway.
This year to save stinging tears

I'll share it with someone special.
Last Christmas I tried not to swear
But the very next day I did anyway.
This year my dear potty mouth
Will come out with something special.

Last Christmas I tried not to leak
But the very next day I did anyway.
This year to have no wet pants
I'll shove in there something special.
Last Christmas I said I would pluck
But the very next day I didn't give a fuck.
This year I'm growing a beard
And that will be really special.

Christmas Time, Menopause and Wine
(Based on the song *Mistletoe and Wine* written by Jeremy Paul, Leslie Stewart and Keith Strachan in 1976)

Christmas time, menopause and wine
Ladies sing, "It's large and it's mine."
With hairs on our nipples and wings on our arms
The meno is here with all of its charms.

Christmas time, menopause and wine
Ladies sing, "It's large and it's mine."
With bums that now bellow a tuneless refrain
And joints that are dodgy with aches and with pains.

Christmas time, menopause and wine
Ladies sing, "It's large and it's mine."
With bladders that won't hold a teaspoon of wee

And little old men that now live on our knees.

Christmas time, menopause and wine
Ladies sing, "It's large and it's mine."
With no sleep at night, and exhaustion all day
Murderous thoughts are now coming your way!

'Twas the Night Before Christmas

'Twas the night before Christmas when all through the house
Not a creature was stirring, not even a mouse.
Then suddenly heard, in every part
The menopausal woman let off a fart.
She got out of bed, and groaned as she went
The aches in her muscles had made her all bent.
She looked in the mirror and saw with a shock
Her tash and her beard had now run amok.
She made for the toilet and then had to squeeze
The tweezing of hair made her violently sneeze.
She went in the shower and thought, 'I look neat'
Looked down to discover she couldn't see feet.
Her arms waved around as she towelled herself dry
Her neck joined the ripples, she wanted to cry.
Then she thought to herself, 'I'm here, I'm alive'
I'll get through this meno, and yes I'll survive.
I'll talk to my friends, have a laugh and drink gin
And wait for the next phase of life to begin.
So when it is silent take a minute to think
The meno will end, there is light - just a chink.
Hang on - you'll get through it, come here for a giggle
Have a smile and a laugh, give that flab a good jiggle.

Out, Out Again

A second tale of a girls' Christmas get-together.

Standing in my bedroom and looking in the mirror, in my little red sparkly dress and nude tights, I thought I looked great. I put my silver sandals on (via wrestling with the twatting straps which are now starting to disintegrate as I've had them for so long) and as I was straightening up I noticed hairs sticking through my tights, and visible black ones squashed flat against my legs.

Oh feck!

I hurriedly removed the sandals and changed my tights for very thick, high denier nude ones and looked in the mirror again. I looked like a throwback from the 70s with bright, shiny American Tan legs.

Yuk!

I decided there was only one thing for it. I whipped them off - I say whipped: I mean dragged them off. Those tights were gripping my legs firmer than white knuckles holding the safety bar on a rollercoaster.

I eventually got them off - creasing my dress, snagging the bastard tights with my sparkly bracelet and sweating my make-up down my face - and ran downstairs to the bathroom. One at a time I hoiked my legs up onto the sink (I knew years of ballet would come in handy at some point) slathered them in shaving cream and got rid of Bungle from *Rainbow* - who'd been merrily residing on my lower limbs for quite some time. Since August to be fair.

I thanked God my dress was short and easily moved to allow this manoeuvre. If it had been long and flowy I'd have needed assistance to hold the layers of tulle out of the way for the razor. Nobody wants jagged tulle on a night out - oh the shame.

On bringing my second leg back down to earth I accidentally slipped slightly, knocked the can of shaving foam onto the floor causing it to expel a lovely dollop onto the wall, dropped the towel and farted!

Nice…

The Gauntlet Has Been Thrown Down

Well, M'Lady…I am going out into battle to secure our most treasured prize and bring it home safely forsooth. I will fight off the marauding evil ones, trying to knock me off my trusty steed and take my place at the front of the hallowed line of hope. I will wave my faithful lance for the heavens hath opened and I will use it skilfully to take out the eye of any peasant that attempts to engage me in a nifty gavotte and manoeuvre me to one side.

I may have to stop off at an infamous watering hole for a much-earned goblet of mead - this is simply to provide much needed refreshment and will not end in my good self dancing on the tables and singing ye olde karaoke. Or taking on the role of court jester and entertaining the crowds with my razor-sharp wit and humorous tales of yesteryear.

Once refreshed I will continue my crusade the last few furlongs and secure the treasure.

My trusty steed will then carry me safely back to you and we will place this treasure in the cold cavern of loveliness, to keep it safe until the day of worship is upon us.

Wish me Godspeed my love and I will be on my way…

Bleedin Nora! You're only going to the butchers in the village to collect the feckin turkey!!

Christmas Jumper Day…Errr…

Christmas jumper day except…I don't do jumpers! What menopausal woman in her right mind would EVER wear a JUMPER!!!

None.

Dear Lord, can you imagine the carnage as every woman of a certain age started ripping their jumpers off and flinging them across the room?!

It'd be like a scene in a poor man's geriatric strip club, with all the old blokes panting as they await the appearance of the Spanx!!

Have You Got It?

Hands up who's goes around on December 23rd saying, "That's it! If I've not got it by now, I'm not getting it."

While secretly knowing that if you did discover you had in fact NOT got it, you'll be rushing down to the shopping centre to get it.

Whatever IT is!

FEELING FRISKY

Who Said Romance Was Dead?

I was getting dry after my shower when hubby came in to the bathroom – to get something out of the cupboard.

I looked at him and smiled.

Feeling a bit frisky I slipped one shoulder out of the towel and glanced at him coyly, then followed it with the other. I allowed the fabric to drop tantalisingly down, slowly revealing my boobs. He looked at me appreciatively, as the towel slithered to the floor, and licked his lips – then his expression changed.

Was it lust? Was it admiration? Was it awe?

He opened his mouth to speak the immortal words that every wife longs to hear…

"You've got a long hair growing out from the side of your left nipple."

Toasted Teacakes

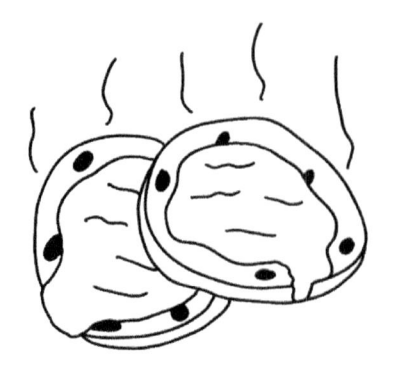

I woke up craving toasted teacakes – no I'm not pregnant, alarmingly that was also hubby's first thought. I chose not to ignore said craving – which would've been the wisest course of action.

So, I changed my pyjama bottoms for tracksuit bottoms, left my pyjama top on, wiped away smudged mascara from under my eyes, slipped my bare feet into crocks, grabbed a hoodie and drove to the shop.

I accidentally wore my close-up glasses instead of the distance ones.

I staggered into the shop, picked up two packs of teacakes and wandered straight into the path of a friend's husband. By the time I'd realised who it was, I was within speaking distance. Had I worn my distance glasses I'd have noticed him early enough to nip down the cold meat aisle and hang out by the salami and bratwurst, until he'd gone. Instead, I had to have a whole conversation with him, whilst going redder and redder at the thought of the state of me.

Why can't I wake up with the urge for quickie morning sex like other people?

Why toasted teacakes?

Not Tonight Jim…

Jim: I'm in the mood to fumble, love.
Rose: Well, how can I refuse?
You make it sound so tempting,
But I can't disturb my snooze.

Jim: What about a quickie then?
Rose: Hmm, lovely though that sounds -
I'm off to meet the girls tonight;
It's quiz night at *The Hounds*.

Jim: Slow and sexy love making?
A big romantic sweep?
Rose: Only problem there Jim is,
You always fall asleep!

Jim: Well, how about a bit of rough,
Laid prone across the table?
Rose: Where's your health and safety Jim?
You know the legs aren't stable!

Jim: I know! We'll do it in a field,
A bit of love 'al fresco'.
Rose: Good God! I'd rather do it in
The freezer aisle at Tesco!

Jim: The car then - snuggled in the back?
Rose: Well now you've lost the plot!
My menopausal flushes Jim
Will make the car too hot!

Jim: The bath? I'll go and pour it now -
My best idea by miles.
Rose: Oh no the water might slosh out
And splash the mosaic tiles!

Jim: The shower then? Yes, that will work
Rose: The cubicle's too small!
My glasses will get broken with
My face squashed up the wall!

Jim: Well shall I go and buy some gear,
Some gadgets and some toys?
Rose: The neighbours will complain though Jim,
Those things make too much noise!

Jim: Let's try a new position then,
They're not just for the young.
Rose: And risk our brand-new mattress, Jim?
Don't think it's that well sprung!

Jim: Right! Sod it! I'm off to the pub!

Let's Talk About Sex…

Let's talk about s…e…x (said in a whisper)

OR

LET'S TALK ABOUT SEX!!!

However you say it, we're going to get into it. Not literally.

Nearly 20 years ago I went to my first Ann Summer's party, hosted by a friend. We all jumped at the chance of the sheer naughtiness of it. Some of us tried on naughty outfits (over our clothes) some of us salivated over naughty DVDs, some of us examined naughty whips, and me? I demonstrated the naughty Clitty Critter - over my trousers, but I still nearly shot through the ceiling when the party organiser turned it on!

Notice my use of the word 'naughty'. Back then talking about sex over our G&Ts was not a regular occurrence. So going to an Ann Summer's party did indeed feel very naughty. Needless to say, much wine was drunk, we stayed until 3am and every single one of us left having ordered the new and exciting Rampant Rabbit.

A couple of days later a few of us actually went into our local Ann Summer's shop - curiosity had got the better of us. We glanced around outside, to make sure nobody we knew would see us entering this den of iniquity, then nervously entered the forbidden paradise. Once inside we avoided making eye contact with the assistants, furtively stroked the fluffy handcuffs, sidled past the impressive display of vibrators on offer (bleedin nora that one would make your eyes water Sharon!) and tried to discreetly glance at the DVD covers - entranced by how the content changed the higher up the shelves you looked. When it was time to leave we cased out the front entrance, then shot out before anyone could see us, quickly bowled into Starbucks and collapsed into giggles.

But now? 20 years later?

I strode into the shop, headed straight over to the Moregasm Rampant Rabbit range, liberated one from its hanging bracket, plonked it onto the counter and walked back out swinging my boldly coloured Ann Summer's carrier bag beside me.

Own your sexual pleasure ladies because…why shouldn't you?

Sex Face

While partaking in a girls' night, and once a few bottles of wine had been knocked back, someone had the fabulous idea of photographing our sex faces when we're in the 'on top' position.

Now I knew this wasn't a great idea. I've looked at my face hanging down into a mirror before (don't ask) and it's enough to give any sane person nightmares. Gravity is a cruel maiden.

At our age, the skin on your face does not cling and stay put when said gravity makes an appearance. Oh no. It hangs off. It hangs off like a sloth dripping down from a tree, whilst clinging on by its fingernails - just. This activity didn't go down well and a lot of squealing and looks of horror ensued. It would appear that seeing bulging eyeballs and slack-jowled skin bearing down on you cannot, in any circumstance, be described as sexy.

I suspect from now on the only sexual position being employed amongst my friends and me will be the missionary.

JOY

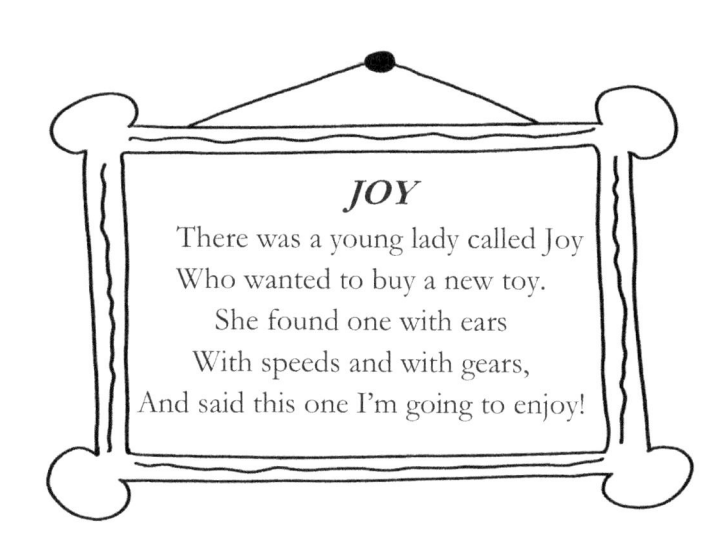

There was a young lady called Joy
Who wanted to buy a new toy.
She found one with ears
With speeds and with gears,
And said this one I'm going to enjoy!

MANDY

There was a young lady called Mandy
Whose man at the beach became randy.
"Don't point that at me"
She started to plea,
"I don't want my 'downstairs' all sandy!"

TRACY

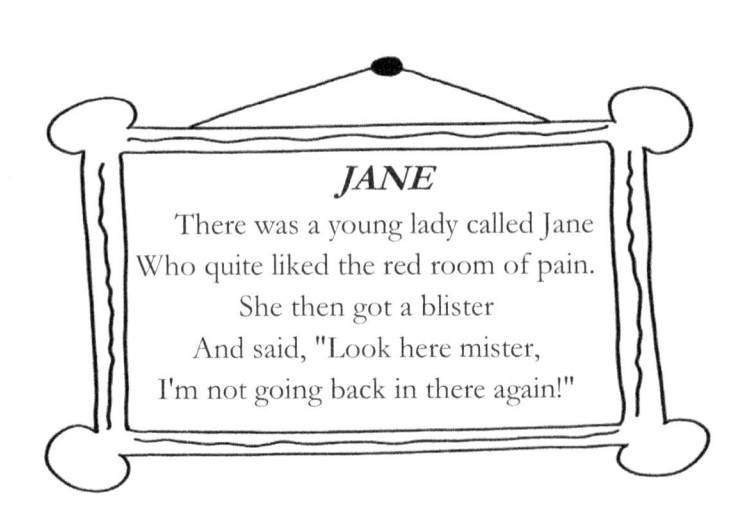

There was a young lady called Tracy
Whose knickers were sexy and lacy.
Til hot with desire
Her knickers caught fire,
And now she wears undies less racy!

JANE

There was a young lady called Jane
Who quite liked the red room of pain.
She then got a blister
And said, "Look here mister,
I'm not going back in there again!"

A GOOD TIME
In my youth, waking up with sore knees, a rosy glow and a bite on my neck meant I'd had a good time the night before...
Nowadays it means I've spent the weekend gardening, forgotten to slap on the factor 50 and omitted to cover myself with industrial strength insect repellent!

MARTHA
There was a young lady called Martha
Going out with a fireman called Arthur.
He gave her a rose
On the end of his hose,
And said, "Baby, you're hotter than lava!"

HERE COMES THE SUN…

Where's the Sun?!

Summer? Pah! WTH is going on?!

Remember those few sunny days in April? That was probably our summer. If only I'd realised at the time. We'd have had every friend round for drinks on the patio, spent full days laying on a sun lounger reading, gone to the beach and had many, many BBQs.

If only I'd known.

Instead of embracing those heady days of sun, I spent them complaining about the heat.

We are never happy with the weather in this country.

Now it feels like someone has burst a giant pipe in the sky, and nobody can find the stopcock to shut off the leak. Does Mother Nature not have the number for a good plumber? I know the gardens needed the rain, but now the plants are waving white flags and waiting for hunky firemen to come along in rescue dinghies.

I can't believe my summer clothes are languishing once again at the back of the wardrobe. All they can do is gaze longingly at the bossy jeans and long-sleeved tops, which have pushed past all the lovely floaty dresses and cropped trousers, to maintain their position at the front again. However, I refuse to go back into boots - even though my cork soled sandals have got trench foot and my white pumps are spending more time in the washer than they are on my feet.

And don't you think we should be able to have a BBQ in summer?! (Said with clenched fists, grinding teeth and manic wild eyes)

It's FECKIN' AUGUST!!!!

Beach Body Ready? Eff Off!

Who told us how we need to look
When laid out on the beach?
Who said our bottoms need to be
 Less melon and more peach?

And who says that bikinis are
The fashion for the young?
Is it because our stomach's flopped,
And boobs aren't tightly sprung?

Some of us have lines of blue
Around our legs so white.
And skin that flaps below our arms;
No longer toned and tight.

Our body's aged; it's seen some life
It's partied, danced, had fun.
And once a year the beach is where
We go to get some sun.

So, no we won't be at the gym,
All sweaty doing weights.
We won't be trying silly diets
Or shrinking down our plates.

We won't be ripping out our hair
With tweezers or with wax.
From places where it's meant to be –
In crevices and cracks.

We won't be buffing up our skin
To get a sun-kissed glow.
We're happy with the way it is,
Although it looks like dough!

We won't be trying to change our thatch
With serums and with creams.
Or trying for the swishy style
That features in our dreams.

We will however hit the beach
Exuding sass and style.
With attitude to do us proud,
A cocktail and a smile!

Speedy Boarding

Human beings…we're all the same.

Speedy boarding…I wonder who invented this little misnomer. You pay to get this preferential treatment, only to discover that so has practically every other bugger on the plane.

If we've gone to the expense of giving ourselves a supposed head start with this little quirk, we will get to the gate as soon as possible and install ourselves as near to the desk as we can; while trying to look nonchalant rather than desperate. This surely isn't necessary as speedy boarding allegedly means that we'll get onto the plane first. Still, we don't want to take the chance that they forget to announce it, or other 'lesser' passengers try and blame ignorance and sneak on at the same time.

Once we've installed ourselves, so close to the front we can see the staff's nostril hairs, we then furtively glance around at all the other people doing the same thing while thinking, 'Are they actually speedy boarding too?' 'I hope they know they'll have to wait if they aren't'

Frankly, it's exhausting.

Move Down the Bus!

When taking the bus from the terminal to the plane, do we get on, use our brains, read the bus and MOVE DOWN?

No. We do not.

We get on the bus, grab hold of the nearest dangling handle, plant our feet in the 'firm stance' position then ignore everyone else as they struggle to get on the bus with us - and struggle even more to squeeze past us. We purposefully stared fixedly out of the window and pretend that we can't feel people getting so close to us we could reasonably expect a medical examination report through the post from them, on our return.

We might step aside if you're trying to get on with a pram, but I wouldn't count on it.

Can You See It, Mildred?

Arriving at baggage re-claim first won't make our suitcase pop out onto the travelator any faster. Just because we're standing there tapping our feet, staring down anyone who has the audacity to think they can squeeze in front of us (whilst wondering if we can leave the kids to keep our space so we can sprint to the toilet) won't make the guys handpick our cases and delicately put them onto the conveyor belt first.

Alternatively, when going the other way, getting onto the plane first won't make it take off any sooner. That plane ain't going anywhere until all the people who were blocked from getting onto the bus, actually get onto the plane!

We're Here, We're Here!

When the plane lands, why do we all instantly jump up? The plane hasn't even come to a complete stand still and we're up faster than a reality 'star' disappearing back into obscurity. If you're lucky you'll have made it out into the aisle and be smugly standing upright; if you were a nanosecond too slow, you'll be standing in the footwell of your seat bent over like Quasimodo.

Whilst holding this position we then start eyeing up the lucky ones in the aisle, wondering which one looks the most likely to let us out. You'll smile so much, at the most obvious candidates, your face will ache the way it did when you were a kid in a battle to see how many gobstoppers you could get inside it.

Lazing around the Pool

Everything a young woman takes to the pool:

- a teeny, tiny glamorous little clutch bag containing a small bottle of suncream spray - one spray used for her entire body – and her phone

- a stylish floppy sun hat

- a look of expectation

Everything I take to the pool:

A mahoosive beach bag containing:

- bottle of water - must keep hydrated, don't want anything becoming more dried out than it already is

- huge bottle of suncream - to regularly slather on and spread with a palette knife

- wet wipes - to remove suncream from hands

- tissues - in case of unexpected sneezing incidents

- pee pads - in case of unexpected sneezing incidents

- painkillers - the last thing I want in the sun is one of my heads

- antihistamine tablets – to help protect from insect bites

- insect bite cream – for when the bites are so twatting big the antihistamine tablets just won't cut it on their own

- purse - none of this paying on your phone malarkey. Phones are for talking, texting and playing Wordle

- plasters – I'm bound to cut something at some point. Probably myself on my razor-sharp wit

- phone - for talking, texting and playing Wordle

- a book…remember those?!

- reading sunglasses for the sun, normal reading glasses for the shade, distance sunglasses for walking around outside, normal distance glasses for walking around inside the hotel (my eyes have struck a deal with the local optician and are now pimping themselves out for free eye drops and a rather nice chain to hold all the bastard glasses around my neck)

- two fans - a paper one for when I want to look sophisticated, a battery operated one for when I'm so effin hot I don't care if everyone round the pool thinks I've brought a twatting dildo with me

- a bloke's sensible sun hat because I need it to actually stay on my head

- a look of resignation

WTF?!

Well, this was embarrassing!

I went for a swim to cool down and was wearing a rather old swimsuit.

I lay down to dry off and for comfort bent my legs up at 90 degrees to my body - then engaged in a bit of harmless phone scrolling.

A sudden breeze had my undercarriage feeling surprisingly draughty…so I put my hand down to investigate.

Turns out that when old swimsuits get wet, they go rather baggy and give up on the job of clinging to you tightly, to protect your dignity when laid down with legs bent up.

Not only was my dignity very much NOT protected, but half my fanny was hanging out too!!

WTF!!

Too Kind, Too Kind

You know the person that makes all the cups rattle in their saucers on the little tables, as they walk past them by the pool?

That's me…that person is me!

I took it as a round of applause, and nodded my appreciation.

Let the Battle Commence

I don't tan. Ever. If I'm lucky I go pink, which frankly isn't actually lucky at all. My arms are prepared to turn a light brown colour, but my legs stoically stay white - white enough to give a hairless polar bear a run for his money.

Actually…talking of hair, which I know we weren't - I digress - my legs are now in need of a re-touch shave as there is stubble on my shins and spider's legs making an escape bid from my knickers. I can almost hear the chief spider rounding the troupes up and organising manoeuvres to escape down my inner thighs…

Anyhow…back to white legs. Every year, round the pool on holiday, I watch people reach for their sunglasses when I walk past. So, this year I decided to use a self-tanning moisturiser. Genius!

I started it a few days before we went away, and by the time we left for the airport my legs had turned a lovely shade of biscuit. Think subtle shortbread as opposed to full on ginger nut.

Once in the hotel room, wearing my tankini and looking at my legs in the mirror, I thought, 'looking good!' So, each day I kept applying the magical moisturiser and admiring my legs. Swanning around the pool like a slightly bronzed babe (in my head) I was. A slightly bronzed babe who'd clearly kept her top half inside all summer, but had sent her legs out into the sun. Slightly mismatched but hey-ho.

However, by day four I started to notice that something strange was happening. My lower legs and thighs were alarmingly going back to their usual bright white self! WTF? I exclaimed loudly to hubby! We both stood and studied my wayward lower limbs and came to the conclusion that the bastard suncream had declared all-out war with the self-tanning moisturiser. Because

I burn so easily, I slather suncream on as if I'm plastering the inside of the Sistine Chapel.

The self-tan had obviously decided it was not a war worth fighting and had buggered off. Except for my knees and ankles…These were two strongholds it was not prepared to give up - like Custer's last stand…on my effin legs. I mean, seriously! If you're going to give up, like the coward that you are, at least take all the stragglers with you. Never leave a man behind and all that!

So…I ended up with brown knees, brown ankles and white legs in between. Think of a zebra crossing but with blotchy peanut butter coloured stripes instead of black and you'll get the picture…

Visiting Satan's Arse

Every year on holiday, in a one-piece bather, I dread going to the toilet. The poolside cubicles are the temperature of the inside of Satan's arse and so tiny that during the 'after care' you invariably graze your arms on the artexed walls.

And THEN you add in a WET all-in-one bather.

AND a hot flush…

First you have to ROLL the bather down - that's the only way that fecker will move. Then you have to TRY and roll it back up again.

OMFG!!

Last time I did this - with my newly acquired menopausal weight - I absolutely could NOT get it back up again! I nearly had to call for help as I only managed to pull it up onto my arse. Not OVER my arse...ONTO my arse! Not even the sweat of a hot flush helped it slide up my body. The hotter I got, the more I panicked. The more I panicked, the hotter I got.

It was a vicious cycle of menopausal hatred and wet bather despair.

After five more minutes of sweating and struggling I'd managed to stretch the top half up to my boobs - just. But there was no way the straps were going to reach my shoulders - that was a step too far for my recalcitrant bather.

So, in desperation I threw my kaftan over me, clutched the top half of the soggy bather to my boobs and thanked God the kaftan was long enough to cover the bottom half - which was now dangling down between my legs like a pair of soaked-to-capacity incontinence knickers.

I waddled up to our air-conditioned room, lay down on the cold tiled floor, wriggled out of the bather and flung it into the furthest corner!

So now? I've swapped to a tankini: big knickers that sit happily over my belly, and a top that comes down far enough to avoid the danger of it riding up, revealing my belly and scaring all of the young children in the nearby vicinity.

At last, I can go to the poolside toilet without partaking in a gym workout. I don't have to sit looking at my naked rolls of fat fighting for space on my knees, and I don't need to do the waddle of shame back to our room.

Marvellous!

It Won't Come Off!

I knew I shouldn't have got so cock-a-hoop about changing to a tankini, because it appears they come with issues of their own too.

On one occasion I got stuck in a wet tankini top and had to get hubby to rescue me from it. That fecker had me well and truly trapped…arms up straight and boob part pinning my shoulders up near my ears.

A panic attack was fast approaching as I bounced against the bed and ricocheted off the wall.

Thank God hubby was there, otherwise I'd have been left thrashing around on the floor like a beached whale out of water, getting hotter and hotter, sweatier and sweatier and still no nearer to releasing myself from the Lycra of doom!

I Nearly Died, There!

You'll be pleased to know I've discovered that I need to extricate myself from my tankini top downwards over my arse, instead of upwards over my head. This works like a dream.

I've been saved from being found on the floor of the hotel room with a look of panic and bewilderment on my face, a bandeau of Lycra around my chin, my boobs looking distinctly mortified (if boobs had eyebrows they'd be raised to the heavens) and my arms trapped upwards like the tufted top of a pineapple!

Not a nice way to leave this world, in a sadistic Lycra based incident…I certainly wouldn't have been remembered with any ounce of dignity Whatsoever.

Get Your Fingers Ready

Who decided that tankini/bikini tops need removable pieces of padding?!

Having washed mine after the holiday, I then had to spend ages with my finger inserted through the tiny opening, as far in as I could get it, trying to unscrunch and unfold the effin' things to get them back into their intended place!

I don't know if I've got it right because I can't tell…but if I've got it wrong, next year by the pool I'll have the left boob going one way searching for a sun lounger and the right boob going the other way searching for a very large cocktail!

And I know which boob I'll be following…

This Way or Segway?

We once offered the teens the chance to choose a family activity. Their choice was Segways. What?!

Exactly…

Naturally the teens took to it like ducks to water; their parents were more like two old turkeys that had inadvertently fallen into a pond.

The training and 'nursery' session was great. Once we'd got the hang of it, we loved it. The wide-open lanes were simply magnificent! Hubby and I were zooming along at 12 miles an hour with the best of them.

Believe me – that was fast!

Having been 'trained' and introduced to it gently, we went away for lunch and decided to go back for the 'adventure' session. I know! How foolhardy! This was billed as rather more 'off-road' and 'hard-core'.

Ridiculous! How much harder could it be?!

Much harder, it turned out.

Instead of wide-open lanes we were plunged into ~~Bear Grylls style terrain~~ the forest. I feared we were going to end up needing some highly technical survival kit and was already furtively glancing around for discarded snake skins to pee into – just in case we had to drink our own urine to keep ourselves alive. If there was some kind of zombie apocalypse, the Co-Op that was only 10 minutes away would inevitably get wiped out leaving us with no cans of cola, lemonade or bottled water. I prided myself in the knowledge that I'd be ready.

The teens zipped in and out of trees, up and down hills, along narrow paths, round hairpin bends and through streams like they'd been doing it all their lives.

We, however, did not.

Every twist and turn I saw my life flash before my eyes. Every tree became an obstacle of death, every inch deep stream an opportunity to drown. And I'm convinced I saw a boa constrictor lurking in the undergrowth – watching and waiting for me to fall off…

I was extremely glad of the pee pad I'd wedged securely into my knickers before setting off.

At one point I managed to wrap myself around one particularly aggressive, objectionable tree and had to be rescued by the instructor. Just as I'd re-gained my equilibrium, a shout went up from the rest of the group as hubby had overplayed the reverse technique, shot forwards and promptly fallen off his Segway - backwards. He landed in an ungainly heap on the floor – legs akimbo, Segway wheels spinning helplessly in the air.

A while later (would it never end?) we had to go down what I thought looked like a very, VERY, steep decline. Naturally I point-blank refused. Nothing was going to get me down that sheer drop on two uncontrollable and slightly stroppy wheels. The instructor had different ideas and declared he was having none of that refusal malarkey. He then, in a rather ungainly manner, dragged me down said ~~cliff~~ slight slope, squealing for the entire length – all 2 metres of it.

I re-joined the group – who were patiently waiting for me to stop faffing around. The teens were torn between laughing hysterically and hanging their heads in shame.

I girlishly giggled and explained that hubby and I were merely fulfilling our job description as parents: embarrassing our kids in as many ways as is humanly possible.

Today was number 55 on the long list of opportunities that life presents midlife parents to do just that.

Job done I'd say!

Good Luck!

Don't you just love it when rain is threatened so you eat inside instead of outside, but it's still really hot.

You have your meal then get up from the table to find that your dress is damp and wrinkled and has moulded itself to your arse like a dodgy politician clinging to power when he's been discovered getting up to no good in a public toilet!

Good luck surreptitiously peeling that mother from your sweaty betty!!

Carry on Camping

Camping…I love the idea, but hate the practicality of actually doing it.

The journey, to the campsite of shattered dreams, was always fraught with fighting teens in the back of the car. The upright bag, which was so big it had to sit between them - and warranted its own seatbelt - would constantly lean to one side. This would invariably elicit outraged cries from the squashed teen blaming the other one for pushing it.

The car would be so rammed full not even a gnat's dick could be squeezed in to join us on this jolly outing. In fact, I don't know how the car realistically managed to move. The boot would be full, the roof box would be full and every feckin' inch of the internal space would be full. I usually ended up with a cool box by my feet, a pillow on my knee and a boy's foot in my back. My seat would be moved so far back, to accommodate the cool box, I'd be practically sitting on the boys' knees.

When we'd finally arrive – frazzled and extremely irritated – it would take two hours to erect the tent from start to finish. TWO HOURS! And finish meant sitting at the wobbly fold out table with the wine box open and a full glass of wine in my hand.

Each time we ~~put ourselves through this torture~~ went away for a lovely family camping weekend I was always determined that I wouldn't get irritated and lose my temper with hubby. But, when it got to 7.30 on a Friday night and the wine box hadn't even left the car, never mind made it to the table, my patience would be running a little thin. Gritted teeth and forced politeness, by this point, would be out in force.

"Would you like me to shove this pole through opening A or would you rather I shoved it up your arse – darling?"

"Could you hold the canvas taught sweetheart, before I wrap it around your neck?"

The tent would eventually make it into an upright position. However, by this point hubby and me would both be limp, barely speaking to each other, communicating via the medium of snarling and racing each other to the bastard pub - leaving the now warm wine box languishing in the bloody car footwell!

Teeny, Tiny Boats

My hubby and boys love being on the water. I, on the other hand, hate it (I might make an exception for a cruise ship sailing around the Med.)

The last time the three of them persuaded me to accompany them on a lake, in a miniscule motorboat, I thought I was going to die. I particularly don't like it when the boat is tiny, when the two teenage drivers purposefully head for the waves created by bigger passing boats, when they change over steering whilst the boat is still moving and when they insist on taking their hands off the wheel and standing up to look at passing landmarks.

So, husband and boys went off in their life jackets to engage in this activity while I went off to a coffee shop to read my book.

When they returned, we headed off for afternoon tea. We chose a traditional looking tea room, so I was rather taken aback when my fruitcake arrived in a plastic packet. Strange. And not really acceptable. Eldest chose a chocolate torte and after poking at it with his fork for a few minutes - with absolutely no preamble – loudly declared,

"This cake is as dry as a nun's fanny!"

The three of us nearly spat out our cakes laughing.

See, we do enjoy family activities together, after all…

For the Love of All Things Shower!

Hotel owners…pray answer me this. What the buggery bollox use is a shower head attached to the wall, or even worse the fecking ceiling?!

It may LOOK stylish but I can assure you it's about as much use as a thong trying to take control of a muffin top! How am I supposed to rinse my fandango with that?!

"Hello reception…please would you send help. My wife did a handstand in the shower, slipped on the wet floor, farted, peed and suffocated herself with her tits!!!"

Please stop this ridiculous nonsense immediately.

HUBBY HOW I LOVE THEE

Battle of the Duvet

Hubby and I once had an all-out fight with our duvet, which resulted in us both helplessly crying with laughter…

Our duvet was still in winter mode, so it was made up of two layers attached at the corners with press studs. I went up to bed one night and noticed there were lumps under the cover. On closer inspection I found that the top layer seemed to have developed a life of its own and was hosting its own private party, throwing all sorts of shapes and quite possibly on the gin. 'I'm not having this!' I thought and immediately began to unbutton the cover to investigate.

I stuck my hands in to have a ferret around and try to straighten the top layer in one particular corner. But it was all bunched up, folded in on itself and REALLY IRRITATING me! (I should mention here that during my years of PMT I really suffered with irritability and inanimate objects would often throw me in to a rage. I'm not convinced it's completely gone…)

I struggled for a while until eventually hubby appeared. He was quite taken aback to find me half inside the duvet cover, red in the face and swearing.

"Aaaargh!" I cried, "There's something wrong with the duvet and I'm having a nightmare!"

"It's alright love," he said, calmly scooping the duvet up, "You just have to hold it up at the edge, hang it vertically like this and shake everything down. It'll sort itself out, you'll see."

"Ok," I replied. "Phew! I'm going to clean my teeth," and off I went. He smiled serenely at me as I passed him. Looking like a man in control of his life, the situation and certainly a stroppy duvet!

Five minutes later I returned to the bedroom, walked through the door and was met by a scene that caused me to burst into uncontrollable laughter.

Hubby had taken his top off and was half inside the duvet cover, red in the face, and swearing as he wrestled with the exact same corner I'd been wrestling with not five minutes before.

"What on earth?!" I spluttered through the laughter!

"Aaaargh!" he exclaimed, "There's something wrong with the duvet and I'm having a nightmare!!!"

Tears were now pouring down my face at the sight of him in a semi-naked tussle with our bedding.

From within the folds of fabric I heard him splutter, "I wasn't happy with it; it was annoying me so I took my top off and decided it needed a damn good seeing to!"

I collapsed in a helpless heap of laughter on the floor, unable to be of any assistance whatsoever. He collapsed on the bed and joined in the laughter.

We gave up in the end and just went to bed. But before I finally went to sleep, I kept remembering the sight of him and bursting out laughing. It just kept bubbling up inside me and I tried to remember the last time I'd laughed long and hard like that. It did me the world of good

Choosing a Jacket

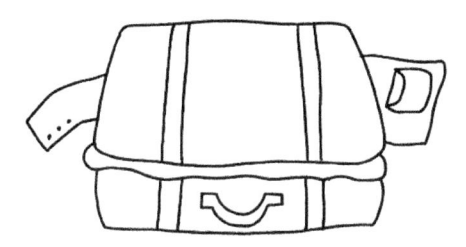

We were in a hotel room packing to leave. I was wearing my small cream jacket, and into the case I was trying to fit my much bigger, brightly coloured bonkers jacket - it's covered in multi-coloured flowers and I adore it.

I was having to try and fold the much bigger jacket and squeeze it into our small over-night case, without creasing it. Much harrumphing and sighing was going on.

Hubby then helpfully suggested that I wear the bigger, bonkers jacket.

Oh. My. Lord!

The green in the bigger jacket DID NOT match the green in my dress, and the style of it was completely wrong for said dress. The two together would make me look like a reject from a 1970s commune, wearing clothes handed down to me from a much larger aged aunt!

Men! Pah!!

You DO Know!

How I watch a film with my hubby...

Me: Ooo do you recognise him?

Hubby: Yes

Me: You don't do you...

Hubby: No

Me: You do! Ooo what was he in...

(Frantically Google's the cast list, finds actor in question, goes to Wikipedia, scrolls down list of what he's been in, finds something I recognise)

Me: That's it! He was in xxxxxx!! Now do you recognise him?

Hubby: Yes

Me: You don't do you?!

Hubby: No

Me: OMG! You DO recognise him! He was in that thing about the woman and there was a dog by a lake…and there was a guy in it that was in that other thing!

Me (looking back at the TV): Who's that? Why's he doing that? What's going on?!

Hubby: FFS! Watch the effin' tele!!

Me: Alright! Oo oo oo…now you DEFINITELY recognise THAT woman!

Hubby: &@*#% off!!!

Do You Think They'll Stock…

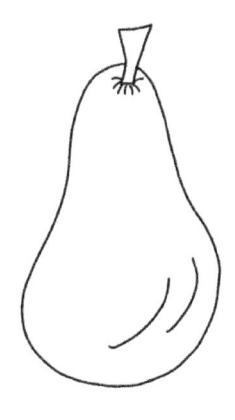

My hubby likes to cook. At the weekend he likes to read a broadsheet newspaper. And he particularly likes to combine the two – by using recipes he finds in the broadsheet's magazine.

The recipes invariably contain somewhat 'out there' ingredients: French rock salt in a dinky, stylish, expensive jar as opposed to table salt in a massive, plastic, economy tub.

I was writing the shopping list. Hubby was reading the broadsheet magazine. He looked up. "Darling…" I knew what was coming, "Do you think the supermarket will sell quinces and malt powder?"

I went to the supermarket in question, to do the weekly shop. Did they stock these two items? Did they buggery. I looked around for replacements, and did the best I could.

I bought him a pear and a jar of Horlicks…

The Time Has Come…

I finally managed to talk hubby into buying new jeans. He'd only had the last lot for 10 YEARS…so actually I'd done quite well getting him to agree to a wardrobe update so soon! He said he needed two pairs in total. I said he needed two pairs for 'every day' PLUS two pairs for 'going out'.

Eyes were rolled…

I hit the shops with a look of steel in my eyes. He hit the shops with a look of fear in his eyes. I knew there was limited time before he refused to drop his trousers anymore, so I quickly headed to the first shop. Hubby veered towards COMFORT fit, I veered towards SLIM fit. We compromised and met at STRAIGHT fit.

I selected several in the same size…but different brands. He selected ONE and declared that all jeans of the same size would fit the same…regardless of brand. Oh dear, how little he knows about clothes shopping. I managed to force another pair into his hands, as he rushed past me into the changing rooms with his solitary pair.

So – two pairs of the same size, but different brands, had made it in. First pair made him speak with a squeaky voice; second pair needed braces to keep them up. My point was made. He agreed to try on ALL of my selection…

ONE pair out of the six he'd taken in was deemed acceptable – by me. Left to his own devices he'd have bought the first pair that vaguely fitted, then legged it.

Went on to the next – and final – shop; remember there was a very small window of opportunity before boredom set in. However, something strange seemed to happen between the first and second shop – hubby suddenly got into the swing of things and started picking up jeans with enthusiasm. AND willingly trying them all on. AND announcing he wanted to buy them...ALL!

So, a successful outcome all round. A wardrobe brimming with up-to-date jeans.

Now all I need to do is persuade him to throw out all the OLD ONES!

Feckin Turn Over!

The scene: Hubby in bed, on his back, snoring...

Me: Sweetheart, please turn onto your side - you're snoring.

Hubby: Ok (lifts arm above head, continues to snore)

Me: Err love, please turn onto your side - you're snoring.

Hubby: Ok (turns head to one side, continues to snore)

Me: Sweetheart...you have to actually move...onto your side.

Hubby: Ok (moves legs, continues to snore)

Me: (coughing loudly) SWEETHEART! PLEASE TURN ONTO YOUR SIDE...YOU'RE SNORING!

Hubby: Ok (fidgets, turns onto his side then flops onto his back. Continues to snore)

Me: OY! TURN. ONTO. YOUR. SIDE. YOU. ARE. SNORING!!

Hubby: Stop waking me up...I was asleep! (Continues to snore)

Me: (pushing him really hard) FECKING TURN ONTO YOUR SIDE - YOU'RE TWATTING SNORING!

Hubby: Woah! There's no need for that...you only had to ask!

Just in Case

The worst hoarder in our house is my hubby. Everything I want to chuck out, he wants to keep...in the garage...just in case.

Just in case what?!

Just in case there's suddenly a national shortage of biscuit tins with damaged lids, empty dried fruit tubs, chunks of polystyrene, dried up tins of paint, bins full of wood and surplus shelf widgets from Ikea furniture?

If there is ever such a shortage, he will most certainly swing into action and save the day.

Until then – chuck it in the fecking bin!!

What Size?!

Hubby went to the butcher to order the Christmas turkey. I'd told him the weight we wanted: 13lb

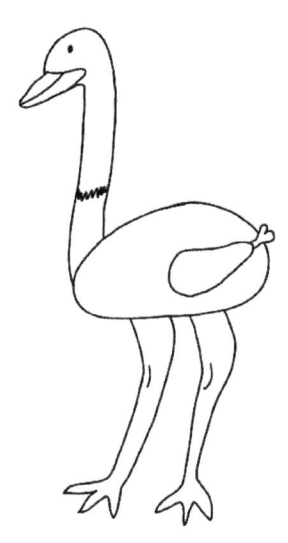

He got to the butcher's and explained he'd like to pre-order the turkey.

Butcher: What size would you like?

Hubby: 13 kg

Butcher: Are you sure about that?

Hubby (*getting hot under the collar, starting to sweat, and wondering why his request was being questioned*): Errr ---yes. Why?

Butcher (*completely deadpan*): Because 13 kg is an ostrich…

Can You Run?

Hubby and I were going into town on the bus for a meal. The bus was late. I hate being late. Hubby assured me it would be ok.

Hubby: It'll be fine…can you run in those boots?

Me: Yes…but I can't run in these knickers! There isn't a pee pad in the world large enough to accommodate me and the word 'running' turning up in the same sentence!

How Do I Look?

Menfolk!

Tell us we look gorgeous, sexy, sophisticated, lovely, beautiful etc.

Do not tell us we look smart!

When a woman has spent ages getting glammed up for a night out, she does not want to be told she looks like she's going for a job interview!!

Err…What?!

Interesting conversation with hubby while he cooked dinner…

Hubby: It says add brandy

Me: huh-huh

Hubby: Shall I do that?

Me: Err…yes…can't you find it? It's in the cupboard by the cooker

Hubby: Yes…but it says 'optional'

Me: hahahahahahaha

In NO part of my brain does 'alcohol being optional' EVER register!

Spider

I was watching TV one night when out of the corner of my eye I saw something move. The cat jumped up and shot over to it. It was running fast along the skirting board (the thing, not the cat), and was so big I thought it was a mouse!

My legs immediately retracted under my body - it's a knee jerk reaction; the same reaction I have to snakes or worms, as I explained earlier.

Anyway, this thing moved away from the skirting board with the cat following it and I could clearly see it was a SPIDER! A spider so big I'd clocked it while watching TV and heard it as it scuttled!

Hubby came running with a glass and both cats sprang into action: one was brave and chased it into a nearby shoe, the other was terrified and sat watching it from a safe distance.

Useless pair!

Hubby eventually caught it and chucked it outside. It was so big it practically asked me to budge up on the sofa and make it a cup of tea. In fact, I'm sure it was wearing a couple of odd socks that had disappeared from the washing basket a couple of weeks ago. It might even have been carrying a few random Tupperware lids.

I spent the rest of the evening walking around the lounge very tentatively, in case it had a whole family living here just waiting to launch a take-over bid on the house.

Towels

Where do you stand on the subject of towels?

I like them tumble dried so they're soft, fluffy and it feels like I'm being enveloped in a cloud.

Hubby likes them dried outside so they're hard, won't fold unless you crack them first and it feels like you're exfoliating your skin with a cheese grater.

What Bag?

Hubby and I got trapped in a shopping spiral the other night - as you do…

For several reasons we've had to move to online shopping, and when it arrives we need to receive it in the garage. We have indoor cats and can't risk losing them, as they whizz past the unsuspecting delivery driver at the front door…giggling like maniacs and sticking their furry fingers up at us as they go.

Hubby was collecting the crates and bringing them in from the garage threshold. Then together we were unloading them into our waiting canvas shopping bags. This was going swimmingly, until hubby suddenly couldn't understand why the bag he'd been filling was getting emptier and emptier, rather than fuller and fuller. Every time he turned his back to collect another crate, he'd return to find his bag looking rather depleted.

"Where's the shopping going that I'm unloading into this bag?" He enquired in a rather bemused tone.

"What bag?" I asked helpfully.

"This bag!" he replied while pointing down at one of the canvas bags.

"It's going into here," I answered, pointing down to my own canvas bag.

"Why? Where do you want it to go?"

"Oh, FFS!" was muttered, accompanied by a face plant emoji.

Turned out that as quickly as he'd been filling up his canvas bag, I'd been emptying it out into another one.

Brain fog right there ladies. Right…there…

Friends, Eh?

We had a rather rude awakening one morning at 5.30am.

A mad axe man came flying in through the bedroom window, a tree in the garden crashed down onto the garage and the ceiling fell down in the bathroom.

Hubby immediately leapt out of bed to go and investigate which bit of this complete carnage he should tackle first. I cowered beneath the duvet having shouted, "Be careful, love," before he left the bedroom. No help whatsoever.

Having searched every room to try and locate which of the aforementioned events had actually happened, he eventually alighted on a small wooden plaque which said, 'If friends were flowers, I'd pick you'. It had slid down from its resting place, against the window in the spare room, and fallen onto the wooden floor.

You might pick me as a friend love but I'd prefer it if you didn't try and give me a heart attack in the process.

Up a Tree Without a Paddle

Hubby decided to prune one of the trees in the back garden. Half way through he'd needed a new blade for his saw, so off I popped to the DIY shop. There'd been an accident between two cars en route so my progress was rather delayed, which meant I took a lot longer than I'd intended. Coming home I went a different way to avoid the blockage.

The whole time I'd been away it had been torrentially raining. I didn't fret about how long I'd taken though, as I knew that hubby would've gone inside to shelter – when I'd left him he hadn't been wearing a waterproof jacket.

Eventually I got home and drove past our house, to discover hubby sitting in the tree looking like a drowned rat – and not a waterproof jacket in sight. He'd apparently cut off a rather large branch which had landed on his step ladder and knocked it out of reach. He was basically stuck up the tree with his legs dangling down like a mewling kitten being dragged away unceremoniously by its mother.

I avoided him seeing me laughing by going inside to 'change into my scruffy jeans' so I could help him. Quite tactful of me that. Once I'd closed the front door behind me, I laughed hysterically to the point where I'd had to visit the loo. Not quite so tactful, but at least he couldn't see me.

I resisted the urge to take a picture of him and send it to our friends via What's App – but only just.

So again, all things considered, I think he got off lightly.

> **CAKE DECORATING**
> I was decorating hubby's birthday cake with hundreds & thousands. Dropped the tub all over the floor and watched helplessly as they turned into millions & trillions…

All Spice…Old Spice…Spice Girls?!

Once again hubby had discovered a recipe in his broadsheet newspaper that he wanted to have a go at: homemade mulled wine. Now, every year we buy a mulled wine spice mix, add red wine, orange juice and brandy and it's lush. This year he decided that he wanted to make the spice mix himself. So, he sent me off to the supermarket for the weekly shop with all spice berries on my list.

What? Exactly.

My raised eyebrows when he made this request told him everything he needed to know about my opinion on this - incredulous at least and stark raving bonkers at most.

So, I dutifully trawled the appropriate shelves looking for said elusive berries – to no avail. Obviously.

I texted him:

Dear Client,

It is with regret (and a certain amount of 'I told you so') that I write to inform you that all spice berries are unavailable – if they even exist. Might I suggest you contact the editor of your broadsheet newspaper who I'm sure will have a direct link to a posh deli in London, which in turn will have a direct link to the posh source of your recipe ingredients.

If this little exercise proves to be fruitless (pun intended) then I recommend that you stick to the usual Schwartz sachet of mulled wine mix that has done the job every year since we got married.

Regards,
Stop Asking Me to Find Bonkers Ingredients.com.

BOTTLE OF WINE

Hubby: Shall we make this bottle of wine last two nights?

Me: Hahahahahahahahahaha!

I NEED A DRINK

You Call That Wine?!

Went to the local pub quiz with the girls – just to reinforce the venue, I did say PUB quiz.

We got there early to stock up on alcohol and went to the bar to order what would be the first of several bottles of red wine.

Isn't that what a pub's supposed to serve? Wine?

They had two bottles – no, not two bottles behind the bar, and the rest in the cellar – two bottles in the entire pub.

Aghast looks were passed between us. To add insult to injury, one of the bottles we were being offered was half empty. So, the reality of the situation was that they had one and a half bottles of red wine – on the entire premises.

I asked how long it had been open, to which the answer came back, "No idea."

Helpful.

"I'd like to taste it please," I requested.

A glass was produced and a mouthful poured in. This small amount was tipped into my mouth, registered on my taste buds then promptly spat back out again. Nice vinegar for your chips love, but under no circumstances could that noxious liquid you're trying to fob us off with be described as red wine.

We ordered G&Ts instead, forced down several packets of cheap crisps and came last in the quiz. We won't be returning again.

The Nana Nap

Is it wrong to want a nap
And have a little sleep?
Just a quick one – 40 winks
No time to count damned sheep.

I've made it half way through the day
A rest is well deserved.
It helps to charge my batteries
And keep me well preserved.

It's not because I'm middle-aged
Oh no, no, no, no, no!
It's just to help me carry on
And keep my youthful glow.

My raison d'etre, joie de vivre
Tiring va-va-voom.
All need the chance to take a break
And in a darkened room.

It won't take long to perk back up
Be fabulous once more.
Just leave me here a little while
Creep out and close the door.

Ok I'll stop the nonsense now
I need it cos I'm knackered!
I went out with the girls last night
Drank cocktails and got hammered!

Slut Dropping Like a Good Un

I love a slut drop.

You can't beat dancing at a party until the wee small hours - and the slut drop has kind of become my thing at these parties.

I do it because I'm thrilled that in my late 50s I still can - not only can I get down to the ground, but amazingly, I can also get back up again!

My hubby always watches on with an air of quiet alarm – waiting to see if I'm going to topple over into a tray of drinks, a piece of furniture, or if we're outside – an unsuspecting bush. I do none of those things. I carry on strutting my stuff, imagining I'm Beyoncé, and slut dropping with all the finesse of a hippo on speed. The amount of alcohol I've usually consumed by this point certainly helps oil the old joints. Although, rather frighteningly, alcohol can also give you a false sense of your abilities.

In my youth one fateful night, I'd been out drinking and dancing. I came home, carried on drinking and dancing and then suddenly decided to drop down into the splits. I can't do the splits, never have been able to and never will be able to. But, in my alcohol fuelled brain, I imagined myself as a member of *Pan's People,* careering around on the *Top of the Pops* stage as I enthusiastically threw myself into the splits - with gusto.

Queue a torn ligament, agony like I hadn't known the like of before and weeks of rest and physio.

Fortunately, it was the forward splits - if I'd attempted the sideways version, I'd probably have ruptured my fanny!

Spritz Away Baby-Oh

Last summer I discovered a new drink. Not new to the rest of the world but new to me: white wine & soda. Now, I know it dilutes the wine (which is a cardinal sin) but I actually really liked it. It was a long refreshing drink, which in the height of the hot sun was very welcome.

So, I thought I'd continue with my new found drink, but unfortunately had no soda left. I quickly beetled up to our local shop to replenish my stock, only to find the soda shelf completely EMPTY! I accosted (politely stopped) a young man to ask him if there was any more soda 'out back'.

Not a euphemism…

He told me that they'd sold out of it this morning. WHAT?! I proclaimed loudly, barely keeping the desperation out of my voice…WHAT'S EVERYONE DOING WITH IT?!

He looked at me with an 'oh dear, middle-aged woman about to lose it' expression, shrugged his shoulders and offered, "Drinking it?"

Funny…

I remained there for a while staring at the soft drink shelves, wondering what would go with white wine instead: lemonade (too sweet), tonic (only for gin), bitter lemon (memories of Cinzano & bitter lemon in the 70s flashed across my mind), ginger beer (what was I thinking?!), Lilt (had I totally lost my mind?!), Tango (was I really that desperate?) or…wait a minute…maybe I could just DRINK the white wine!!!

Marvellous idea! I hurried over to the fridges, picked up two bottles of vino and left happy.

Who needs new-fangled drinks anyway…cheers!

What the Hell Use is This?

So, which misinformed, delusional and frankly insane person thought that creating a 187ml bottle of wine would be a good idea? 187ML?? What the hell use is 187ml? That's just one glass of wine! Who on earth drinks only ONE glass of wine?!

Maybe it's handy for cooking…utter lunacy! I always buy a normal sized bottle for cooking and use 100ml in the recipe then drink the other 650ml while opening and closing the oven door a few times. For added effect I wear an apron, strut around waving a wooden spoon and occasionally shout out words like sauté, simmer and spatchcock.

Well, it would be rude to leave an unfinished bottle of wine lying around…unfinished bottle of wine?

Seriously?

Is that actually a thing?!

To Wine or Not to Wine...

Drove home from work trying to decide whether or not to open the wine when I got in. I opened the outside porch door to find the inner porch door wide open – I am constantly telling the teens to close this.

I stood on the post – I've lost count of the number of times I've asked them to pick this up when they come in. I tripped over the cat demanding to be fed – both boys were horizontal on the sofas with iPads glued to their hands, impressively ignoring the cat's plaintive cries of hunger (massive headphones clamped over their ears probably helped).

I shouted at them to pick up their blazers, coats and bags dumped in the lounge and take them to their bedrooms. Then I demanded to know if they'd got any homework.

I went through to the kitchen and cleared the table, which was still littered with their breakfast debris.

I listened to three messages on the answer machine offering me compensation money for that car accident I'd been in, the chance to reclaim mis-sold PPI and a whole set of new double-glazed windows.
Easy decision really – the wine was opened!

I'm NEVER drinking AGAIN!!

I go out for a little drink,
And come back home flushed slightly pink.
I spend the next day ill in bed,
With tummy ache and pounding head!

I stagger round – a shade of green,
Being smirked at by the righteous teen.
Pretending that it's just a bug,
Whilst clinging to my coffee mug.

Will someone kindly tell me please,
Why drinking brings me to my knees?
And why that now I'm 50 plus,
My body has become a wuss?

This midlife nonsense is a curse,
This new intolerance the worst.
It seems that now I'm middle-aged,
My coping gene has disengaged!

Dry hair, hot flushes, bulging waist,
And in my mouth a funny taste.
I need some respite, don't you think?
FOR GOD'S SAKE LET ME HAVE A DRINK!!

On a Far-Off Planet Called 'Hangover Hell'

On a far-off planet called Hangover Hell
Sits a middle-aged woman who's not feeling well.
Having drunk like a fish and knocked back the wine

She's still in her jamas and not feeling fine.
Her hair looks like Worzel all over the place
Her stomach is rolling she's green in the face.
The room keeps on tilting, the walls won't stay still
I think she's still pissed and is going to be ill.
She's munching her way through a big bag of Revels
Sitting there dribbling and looking dishevelled.
She's asking herself why on earth did she do it?
Cos she laughed and she giggled all the way through it!
But now she will pay as her youths sit there grinning
As she tries to pretend that the room isn't spinning.
Approach her with care cos midlife's a bitch
Don't talk of her state - she'll turn into a witch.
Sparks will fly from her eyes if you mention her age
"It must be a bug!" she'll shout in a rage.
Just leave her alone and leave her to snooze
Cos everyone knows she now can't take her booze!!

Pop!

I've always been afraid of opening a bottle of bubbly. Not afraid to drink it I might add, just afraid of getting the cork out to actually allow me to drink it.

I reckon this comes from watching too many 1970s slapstick sketches on the television. Every time a bottle of fizz was opened it invariably sprayed its contents everywhere, the cork would fire out and bounce around the room before landing in someone's open mouth or quite often knock out an unsuspecting cat.

So, opening bottles of fizz has always been hubby's job, but today he was out. And I fancied a Prosecco so, loins needed to be girded, a tea towel needed to be wrapped around the bottle and a glass needed to be on stand-by.

I was going in…

And once I'd gone in, I realised why I hadn't gone in before and that I'd never be going in again!

I slowly started to prise the cork out (millimetre by millimetre), leant back away from the top of the bottle, scrunched my eyes shut tight and held my breath until the indomitable cork eventually popped out.

OMFG!

Why didn't I realise that the 1970s slapstick sketches were actually based on reality?!

The cork finally came out with such a loud pop that it caused me to jump, squeal, slosh liquid onto the floor and trip over the cat - who clearly wanted a starring role in this slapstick nonsense I was recreating!

On the upside…at least I got the bastard bottle open!

Cheers!

Hangover…Again…

I had another bloody brilliant night dancing to some banging tunes, and enjoying some rather marvellous red wine.

Unfortunately, the morning after it felt like an army of tiny men were building an extension inside my head, that I hadn't requested. I desperately wanted them to stop arguing with their foreman, who had a really loud bark and was clearly not happy with their work ethic. They'd also brought with them some mates, who were in a boat inside my stomach re-enacting a scene from *The Perfect Storm*.

I decided to just sit very still on the sofa, with the cat on my knee, whilst eating plain crisps and drinking cola - until I felt better.

I did actually manage to stagger off to get more crisps at one point - not too fast otherwise *The Perfect Storm* scene would've suddenly taken centre stage and the massive wave that threatened to capsize their boat would've made an appearance all over the cat!

Miniature of the Demon

A friend gave me a miniature of what I soon discovered to be a VERY strong rum!

I added coke to it and careered around the kitchen with a draining spoon in one hand, a spatula in the other, "Don't You Want Me Baby?" blaring out of the speakers and the cat looking at me with wide eyes and crossed legs; because she daren't go past me to get to the litter.

I stared into the frying pan, wondering what the hell I was making, because I couldn't seem to work out where I'd left the recipe. It was probably in the downstairs loo.

I carried on careering around the kitchen, waving utensils about and marinating myself in the demon rum.

Run pusscat…run!!

The Weekend's Here!

Friday - You're here at last! It's your turn for door duty. You can let Saturday in. Saturday always brings good times and alcohol.

If Sunday turns up that's fine too. Sunday's always good for relaxation.

But under NO CIRCUMSTANCES let that fecker Monday in!!

Gin Pancakes

Ingredients

Flour, milk, eggs, lemon, gin

Method

1. Measure out flour and milk

2. Drink gin

3. Crack eggs into jug and whisk

4. Drink gin

5. Pour eggs into frying pan

6. Drink gin

7. Beat flour

8. Wipe flour from face

9. Drink gin

10. Wonder why frying pan has an omelette in it

11. Toss milk

12. Drink gin

13. Stare at milk on floor

14. Squeeze sugar, and sprinkle lemon onto worktop

15. Serve -with gin

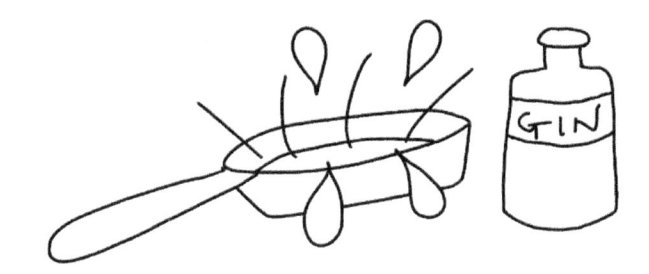

The Gin Dictionary

Ginfluencer: A person who has many gins in their cupboard. They'll offer you one, suggest a flavour they think you'll like, then sit and get drunk with you.

Ginfinity: My ability to drink gin knows no limits

Ginfuriated: Me when I'm told the gin's run out

Ginstructions: Pour gin into glass
                  Add tonic
                  Add ice & a slice
                  Hand to me

Gincident: An outrageous event that happens whilst under the influence of gin

Ginnovative: Pushing the boundaries and adding fruit to your gin

Gindependent: I'll pour my own gin thanks

Ginvitation: A chance to go over and drink someone else's gin

Ahem…

You know when you're so squiffy you forget you're not on your own and lift a butt cheek to let out a corker…then look up from your phone scrolling to remember that you're actually in a restaurant - and there are three other tables of diners looking at you.

That was me…

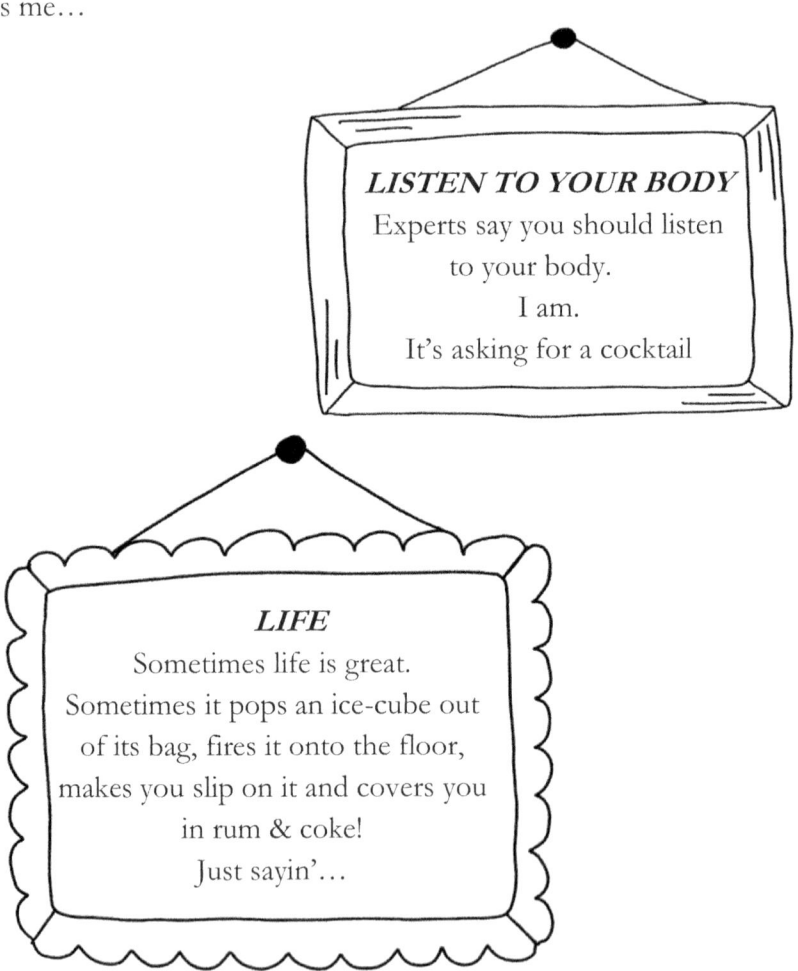

LISTEN TO YOUR BODY
Experts say you should listen to your body.
I am.
It's asking for a cocktail

LIFE
Sometimes life is great.
Sometimes it pops an ice-cube out of its bag, fires it onto the floor, makes you slip on it and covers you in rum & coke!
Just sayin'…

I SAW IT ON THE T.V.

Dearest Gentle Reader,

I bring you excellent news - the new series of *Bridgerton* has returned to our lives bringing with it much jollity, gaiety, promenading, tight breeches, devilish sideburns, lace gloves, lascivious glances, expert ~~whoremanship~~ horsemanship and flirting behind fans.

Prepare your heaving bosom, unveil a new dance card, keep those saucy ankles well and truly under cover and let's skip cock-a-hoop into the Queen's Ball - readying ourselves to stand prettily around the fountainous water feature.

Once in situ we will flutter our eyelashes at any unsuspecting member of the serving staff, who wanders past holding aloft a tray of gins and some mouth-watering nibbles. We shall distract him with our fans then when his attention is drawn, swipe clean his tray and relieve him of his offerings. Before he has had chance to notice any wrong-doings, his offerings will be secreted under the nearest over-the-top rhododendron display, that I will immediately claim as my own. My bush (for goodness sake!) will then become the most popular meeting area for the whole ball and I will smile benignly whilst refusing to move more than 2 cm away from it.

We shall not be fluttering our eyelashes at any menfolk bowing in our direction, dear reader, unless we need one to change a plug. And even then, I am sure we could manage this task ourselves - once we had hoiked our tumultuous layers of undergarments out of the way to allow access to the complete set of Phillips and flathead screwdrivers we keep about our personage in readiness for such a plug socket emergency.

Yours truly,

Lady Gristledown

How to Be a Regency Lady

Here are some hints and tips on being a Regency lady…

Always hoik your boobs up as high as you can, stopping short of letting your nipples escape - it's a fine line between lady and slut. If you cross it, you'll be less The Ton and more The Bigg Market in Newcastle on a Friday night

Use your fan wisely. When warding off a hot flush you could actually be signalling, "I'm up for a bit of loose knicker action behind Big Bert's Fish & Chip shop."

Don't fill your dance card up to capacity. Stay on the right side of interesting and alluring, as opposed to desperate and gagging for it.

Have a new 30' dining table installed. Sit at the opposite end to your other half and enjoy shouting "Pass the wine down!" then feign an inability to hear when they ask for it back.

Practice walking with a straight back and head held high. Walking around the house with a tray of gin & tonics and a bowl of peanuts on your head will help immensely with this endeavour.

And finally, practise speaking correctly and enunciating every syllable to perfection. Less, "Last night we ad a rayt good shag." More, "On the evening before today we partook of a soupçon of insertion, after which we enjoyed tea in the drawing room while he rested his weary eyes and I played a Gavotte on the pianoforte - while embroidering myself a 10" long dildo."

An Unrequested Review of the film *Saltburn*

Firstly…that is so not the best way to clean a bath love. It's Cif Bathroom Spray you want. Your tongue hasn't got enough abrasion and you'll be picking those black mouldy bits, that lurk around the plughole, out of your teeth for days.

Secondly…I hope you've got a bloody good nail brush to get the dirt out of your nails, after scrabbling around in that soil for so long. Can you use said brush on the end of your knob too? Do they make a gentler, less aggressive version for such an occasion?

Thirdly…Lying in the grass naked?! FACE DOWN?! Have you not heard of ticks?! Girls and boys…you do NOT want those little blighters anywhere near your toilet parts!

Fourthly…The night time garden scene…I have no words. Other than to say I might possibly be scarred for life. I will never be able to wipe cherry jam from around my mouth again, without giving myself the dry wretch.

And finally…I don't think I'll ever be able to hear *Murder on the Dance Floor* without thinking I need to do something with those limp bananas that have been languishing at the bottom of the fruit bowl for too long.

Banana loaf anyone?

It's Danglin' on the Dance floor
(Based on the song, *Murder on the Dance Floor* written by Sophie Ellis-Bextor and Gregg Alexander in 2001)

It's danglin' on the dance floor
And you'll probably now catch a cold
Hey hey hey hey
It's flappin on the dance floor
But you'd better use Daz or Bold
DJ - gonna need to wipe those goddam tables down!

I know, I know, I know, I know, I know, I know
I've seen you grind
And so, and so, and so, and so, and so, and so
I've now gone blind!

If you think you're getting away
I will prove you wrong
I'll take you all the way
To put your boxers on
Hear me when I say…

Hey!

It's danglin' on the dance floor
And you'll probably now catch a cold

Hey hey hey hey
It's flappin on the dance floor
But you'd better use Daz or Bold
DJ - gonna need to wipe those goddam tables down!

IS IT ME OR IS IT HOT IN HERE?

Nature at its Finest

If we're quiet we can observe the strange, and often misunderstood, Menopausal Women. She can often be found in her natural habitat: the sofa, in her natural plumage: the dressing gown.

The menopausal woman is a multi-faceted creature capable of impressive multi-tasking: she can sneeze, wee and fart all at the same time.

The hair of the menopausal woman appears thick in some places yet is disappearing at an alarming rate from others; her eyebrows, legs and fanny are balding on a daily basis.

This is because while she is sleeping small creatures from other species come and steal her hair, to make nests for themselves. After a while, when they have finished with the hair, they very kindly return it. Unfortunately, they can't remember where they took it from in the first place. So, to avoid waking the menopausal woman (and facing her anger at being woken from a sleep it took her two hours to get in to) they shove it back onto the first place they see: her face.

Hence the menopausal woman awakes to find a newly acquired luscious beard and moustache. The small creatures who created this masterpiece admire their work, then tiptoe smugly away hoping that she is thrilled with their endeavours. We have it on good authority that, NO - SHE FOOKING IS NOT!

Like the very young of the species, the menopausal woman also suffers with continence issues and also like the very young she has to wear a nappy. Unlike with the very young nobody finds this cute - least of all the menopausal woman herself. Leaking when doing even mundane things, like walking back to her lair from the watering hole, is feckin annoying for her.

The menopausal woman has a very poor memory and at different times of the day can be found sleeping on a different sofa. She's also often spotted wandering around the grasslands trying to find her parked car.

At this point in her life, she starts to lay down extra padding to protect her from inanimate objects that now throw themselves in her direction with evil intent - door handles, sharp corners of dressers and obnoxious table legs all gang up to piss her off. It is also at this point that swear words never uttered before become permanent residents in her vocabulary. There doesn't seem to be any other reason for this extra padding, unless she is evolving into a whale. It's not as if she needs this extra fat to assist with hibernation, although she often thinks that sounds like a bloody marvellous idea.

Her arms are also interesting, as they seem to be turning into wings. Perhaps she is actually evolving into a seagull and will soon be found flying around squawking, crapping on people who annoy her and swooping down to steal their chips.

On the other hand, with all the facial hair she is sprouting, she could indeed be evolving into a yeti. Be aware that if she sits on your sofa you will probably need to use a pet de-fuzzer, to remove all the hair she will inevitably leave behind.

This creature can no longer regulate her temperature. Being engulfed with eyebrow singeing heat can make her very dangerous. She also struggles with supressing the desire to kill other species around her who are behaving like feckin' idiots, or even just breathing. The breathers are the worst.

There is only a female of this species, as the male realised pretty quickly that it couldn't cope with all the shit the female has to deal with.

Always approach the menopausal woman with care…and if you value your life, DO NOT WAKE HER UP!

Oh Menopause, Oh Menopause…

Oh menopause, oh menopause
You're here at last – woohoo!
And all the things I've heard about
I see you've brought them too!

Put your feet up, make a brew
I'm told you're here to stay.
You're going to change my life I guess,
Well that's what people say.

I've heard that there are lots of things
I'm going to get to meet.
So tell me all about it then,
Hang on I'll take a seat.

Red hot flushes
Itchy skin
Running to the loo.
Temper tantrums
Sleepless nights
Not bad, that's just a few.

Oh, sorry did you say there's more
Beg pardon do go on.
I can't help thinking that's enough;
You surely must be done?

Palpitations
Aches and pains
Fluctuating weight.
Feeling anxious
Stiffening joints
Now let me get this straight.

I have to suffer all of this
Because I am a woman?
That's surely just a horrid joke
'Cos most of it's not human!

Night time sweating
Weakened bones
Falling out with friends.
Low libido
Memory loss
How long until it ends??

The years may be as long as ten?
Or maybe only five?
But why do I deserve all this?
And how will I survive?

Nagging headaches
Always tired
Dryness down below.
Irritated
Murderous thoughts
Not sure I want to know!

Feeling dizzy
Painful boobs
Drying skin and hair.
Bloated tummy
Thinning nails
I'm starting to despair!

Don't think I really want to change,
And truly not like this.
It's good you came, but off you go
I'm giving it a miss.

Muscle tension
Burning tongue
Low and tetchy moods.
**I've heard enough
It sounds like hell
So basically, I'm screwed?!**

If women have to cope with this
Then what about the men?
Now tell me all the things THEY get –
NOTHING?! – Say again!!

What's that you say, there is one thing;
They do it to their grave.
They have to tend their facial hair –
THEY HAVE TO FUCKING SHAVE?!

Give Us a Clue

Went on the train to meet friends for a shopping day.

Sat across from a rather gorgeous young student, reading a paper on Organophosphorus Reactions – according to my phone that wasn't even a word. I looked old, menopausal and read *Woman's Own*. Half way through the slew of stories about barmy celebrities, large bottoms and botox I found a crossword. So, I got out a pen to have a go.

I had to give up after completing only FIVE clues.

The intellectual student had the good grace to look away, as I tried to surreptitiously fold the magazine up and slide it back into my bag – while trying to look as though I was bored with such a puerile crossword, couldn't really be bothered wasting my time on it and absolutely had NOT been struggling to do it in the slightest…

Menopausal Pom-Poms

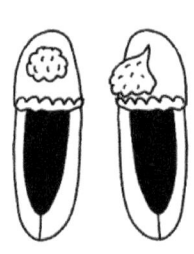

I fear one of the pom-poms on my slippers is going through the menopause: saggy, falling apart and annoyed that the stuffing has dropped to its bottom half - yet hanging on in there, because in its head it's still firm, pert, beautifully shaped and ready to party!

And Another Thing…

Ever sat bolt upright in bed, just as you're falling asleep, because you've remembered something you have to do? Or woken with a hot flush, then can't get back to sleep for thinking about things that need your attention?

I'm always doing it, so last Christmas hubby bought me a lush pressie: A Night Time Notes book.

This got me thinking about the kind of reminders I write in my 50s - compared to when I was in my 20s.

In my 20s I wrote things like:

- sort out lip glosses

- arrange knicker drawer into colours

- walk around the block once a week to keep in shape

- book beautician to define and trim eyebrows

In my 50s I write things like:

- sort out moustache and chin hair

- arrange knicker drawer into categories - big, large & mahoosive

- check if exercise gear comes with a built-in corset

- cancel gym membership - can't find gym gear with strong enough scaffolding

- buy powder or pencil or wax to try and recreate lost eyebrows (probably need all three)

- buy pee pads - might need the actual full-on knickers version

REMEMBER TO USE THE REALLY EXPENSIVE NECK WRINKLE CREAM I BOUGHT TWO MONTHS AGO AND HAVEN'T EVEN OPENED YET!!

Meno Brain Did it Again

Meno brain really had a field day yesterday.

I had to go on a visit while at work and accidentally left my cardi at the venue. I walked home at the end of the day to discover that I'd also not got my key. Hubby was out, I was in only my short-sleeved top, and it was bloody freezing.

I also needed a wee.

Hubby was an hour away and son was at the gym.

I looked around, desperately searching for warmth. Should I go into the back garden and wrap myself in the table cover? Should I crawl under a car and risk being spat at by the local cats, unsure of this new creature lurking in their hiding place? Should I climb into the wheely bin and hope the bin guys didn't come before hubby got home? Should I pop up the street to my young neighbour and demand a toilet, cuppa and access to her sofa?

Or should I do the sensible thing and go round to a friend's…I did the latter.

I walked to my friend's dragging my now fully laden pee pad, shivering torso and chattering teeth with me. Had a lovely warm cuppa, wrapped myself in her proffered cardi and thawed out on her sofa until my son came for me.

I arrived home, walked into the kitchen to start cooking, went back into the hall for my phone - so I could send her a thank you message - and discovered…

I'd left my feckin phone at her house!

FML!!

🎵Oh meno brain, oh meno brain
You've gone and done it once again…🎵

Feeling Hot, Hot, Hot

On one of the hottest days of the year I decided, in my wisdom, to make piri-piri chicken pie. What the actual hell was I thinking?! Three different spices plus chilli powder!

The sweat was pouring down my back, the kitchen was the temperature of a volcano about to erupt (having indoor cats means the window can only be opened to the width of a gnat's dick) and my hair was plastered to my head. My hot flush fan had run screaming into the corner demanding a rise, private healthcare and a bonus scheme…

I then decided that the only way I could cope was to strip down to my bra, big knickers and apron. I quickly closed the kitchen blind as I didn't want to give old Fred from across the way a heart attack.

I warned my sons not to enter the kitchen, as the sight that would greet them would scar them for life.

Although actually, I was tempted to call them in, throw off my apron, fling my arms wide and shout, "Boys! Behold! Feast your eyes on this…for this is what a REAL woman looks like!"

And to eat the feckin pie I had to sit on the chair with the tablecloth wedged up on to the table under a dish, to avoid it coming in to contact with my legs. Hubby fanned my face with a magazine and I fanned my fandango with another!

Next time it's this hot, think effin salad!

Buzzzzzzz…

As soon as I started with hot flushes - I was on it buying fans.

I ordered two from the internet to be ready – I'm a woman who likes to be organised. I bought a Spanish paper one and a small hand-held battery operated one. You can never have too many fans.

I told hubby that when we were at friends' houses if I felt a hot flush coming on, to avoid feeling embarrassed, I'd simply remove myself to the bathroom with my trusty battery-operated fan and deal with it until it passed.

He raised one eyebrow, grinned at me and said, "You'll feel more than embarrassed if you go to the bathroom and the only sound that can be heard through the door is the buzzing of a battery-operated gadget!"

Whose are These?!

I was driving home from the swimming pool and had an itchy leg. I gave it a scratch, then suddenly realised that the stitched seams running down the front of my leggings had disappeared!

"OMG!" I exclaimed out loud, "I've got someone else's leggings on!"

(Not that this is even possible when we're in separate cubicles, but common sense and reason disappear when you're in a blind panic.)

I got home, went into the house and gave the leggings a full investigation.

Turned out they were not in fact someone else's, they were indeed mine, and I had somehow managed to put them on backwards…

Strewth!

A-Z of The Menopause

A – arse - huge and wobbly yet strangely flat & shapeless. What IS that all about?!

B – bingo wings – if ever we need to escape off a mountain top, without the aid of a plane, our arms have got us covered

C – chicken pieces – now residing at the tops of our inner thighs. Delightful…

D – down – where every external body part seems to be heading; particularly our faces

E – eyebrows – thinning by the day except for the rogue 2" long white one now standing out loud and proud

F – fanny – as dry as the Sahara Desert but with less camels – just the odd toe…

G – grumpy – as a dwarf…cute. As a menopausal woman…not so much

H – hair – dropping out of some places, sprouting up in others. Balding eyebrows, head and fanny; luxuriant chin, upper lip and toes

I – incontinence liners – where would we be without them eh? Wet! That's where we'd be!

J – joints – once doing an excellent job of holding our body together, now had a meeting with their union and complaining daily about working conditions

K – knees - heading south; mine are currently half way down my calves

L – lack of memory - what was I saying? Why am I in this room? I'm sorry, but do I even know you?!

M – muffin top - launched an all-out attack on our body and blatantly refuses to be tucked into waistbands: like a wannabe reality contestant trying to take centre stage

N – night sweats – waking up hot…calm down bed sharer, not in a good way. In a 'FML! Why am I now sleeping inside Satan's arse??' way

O – oestrogen – what's that? Am I missing something?!

P – pants – fecking mahoosive!

Q – queen – we are indeed one of these, and deserve the respect that comes with the title

R – removal of hair – well we can but try. I reckon someone is sneaking in during the night and sprinkling fertiliser over my face

S – sex - female. Next question?

T – tummy – hangs down like an apron of fat, sadly doesn't come with a pocket for our phone

U – udder – boobs a cow would be proud of

V – vaginal air bubble – causes us to walk round the supermarket bandy legged, throwing all sorts of shapes and looking like we've wet ourselves trying to get rid of the offending bubble 'naturally'

W - wee – WTAF?! We now pee our pants every time we cough, sneeze, laugh or…walk!!

X – x-rated – our language. On bad days, blue enough to impress a teenager

Y – Y??? – seriously, please someone tell me why men get away scot-free?!

Z – zzzzzzz – elusive, desperately wanted and the stuff of fantasies. Like a unicorn to a 5-year-old

Dear Hot Flush,

Is it necessary to start at my toes, travel up my body until you reach my head, set off a twatting volcano inside me then erupt and pour sweat out of every orifice?!

Please stop making me look like a beetroot on a regular basis; it's very unbecoming and is spooking the cat.

Yours,
Overheating of Oxford

The Menopausal Weather Forecast

Up North is going to be dry, wild and untameable with stormy outbursts. This will cause deforestation in some areas and sprouting of new shrubbery in others.

Down south you can expect damp with wet patches and sudden outbreaks of wind. This will require some members of the population to purchase flood defences for protection against sudden leaks.

And all over there are going to be constant heatwaves sweeping from south to north, causing moistness where it's not required, a feeling of overall discomfort and a national shortage of fans…

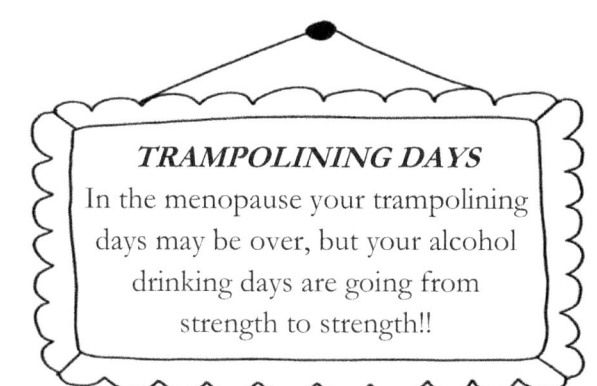

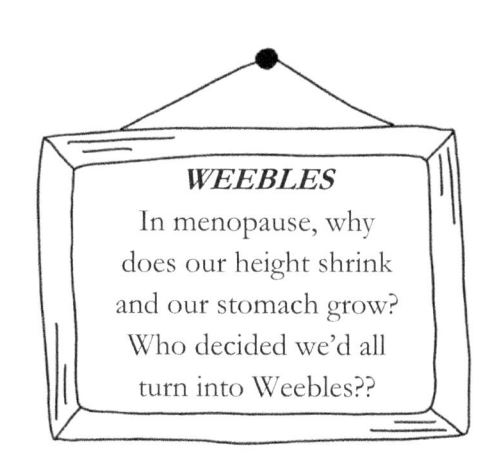

TRAMPOLINING DAYS
In the menopause your trampolining days may be over, but your alcohol drinking days are going from strength to strength!!

WEEBLES
In menopause, why does our height shrink and our stomach grow? Who decided we'd all turn into Weebles??

HEY ALEXA!
Who is this person I'm talking to?
They look familiar, they sound
familiar, they clearly know me but
I haven't got a FECKIN' CLUE
WHO THEY ARE!!!!

SLEEP PATTERN
1am – wide awake
2am – wide awake
3am – wide awake
4am – wide awake
5am – wide awake
6 am – sound asleep
7 am – ALARM!!!!!

THREE STAGES OF A HOT FLUSH

1 – Don't know what you're on about, this seems fine - I'm just glowing prettily
2 – Ooo that's annoying – I seem to be sweating somewhat
3 – OMFG! If I get another hot flush like that I'm going to die!!

STAGES OF A NIGHT TIME HOT FLUSH.

1 – foot out of duvet
2 – leg out of duvet
3 – whole body out of duvet
4 – GIVE ME BACK THE DUVET - IT'S BLOODY FREEZING!!!

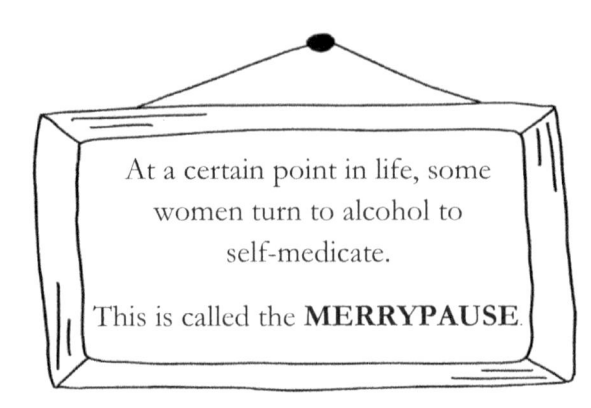

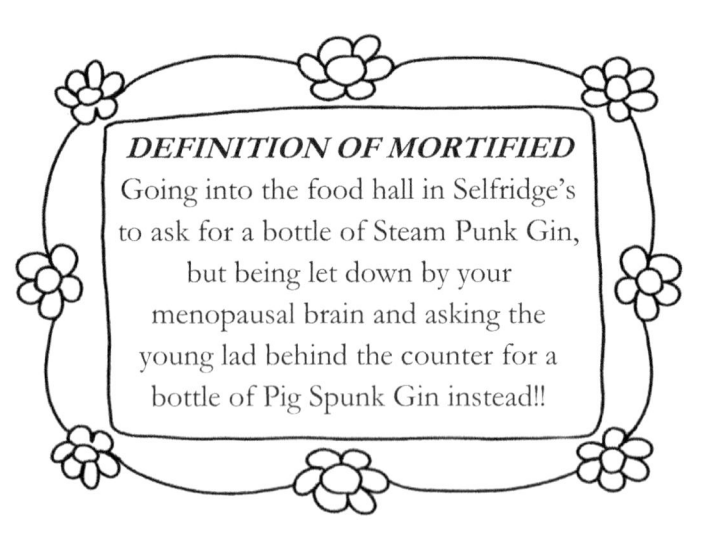

At a certain point in life, some women turn to alcohol to self-medicate.

This is called the **MERRYPAUSE**.

DEFINITION OF MORTIFIED
Going into the food hall in Selfridge's to ask for a bottle of Steam Punk Gin, but being let down by your menopausal brain and asking the young lad behind the counter for a bottle of Pig Spunk Gin instead!!

IN OUT, IN OUT…
Spent last night in bed doing the menopausal hokey cokey…
You put your left leg in, your left leg out, in out, in out…

Shout out to all the menopausal women who've just trumpeted their way downstairs, looked smugly around and thought,
'Yes! That was me…for I am Queen of the Farty Bottom!

Menopausal House for Sale

- Has been alarmingly extended
- Plumbing leaks
- Garden bush needs a good trim
- Outside cladding is a lost cause
- Central heating is stuck on high
- Entrance to basement needs lubrication
- Basement floor is sagging
- Gas is constantly escaping
- All original features

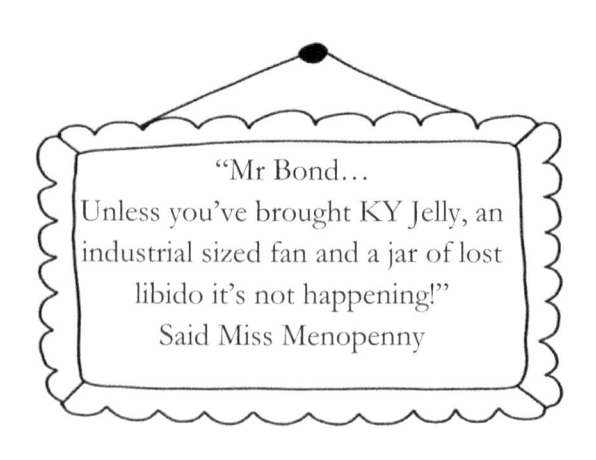

"Mr Bond…
Unless you've brought KY Jelly, an industrial sized fan and a jar of lost libido it's not happening!"
Said Miss Menopenny

Menopausal Car for Sale

- Prone to overheating
- Bodywork needs attention
- Undercarriage is knackered
- Down pipe leaks
- High mileage
- Sat Nav forgets where it's going
- Refuses to move if upset
- Works best when well-oiled

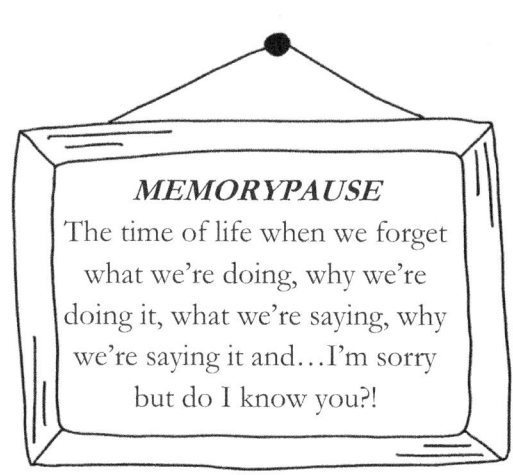

MEMORYPAUSE
The time of life when we forget what we're doing, why we're doing it, what we're saying, why we're saying it and…I'm sorry but do I know you?!

Text Speak for Menopausal Ladies

WTF - Where's the fan?
FML - FAN ME LOADS!!
BFN - Bloody forgotten now...
BFF - Balding frou-frou
BRB - Ballooning rogue belly
BTW – Bring the wine
ETA - Epic tash - alarming!
CBA - Chin beard - alarming!
TBH - These bastard hairs!
ATM - Annoying, twatting menopause!
FYI - FUCK! You're IRRITATING!
ASAP - Always sneeze and pee!
ROFL - Rolls of fat - languishing
PMSL - Literally...

Where Does it Go?!

Just read my HRT instructions:

- stick the patch below the waste
- don't stuck it on your boobs

Contradiction in terms for some of us…

Brain Fog - What is That?

Brain fog? Goodness what is that,
Forgetting where I am?
The butter's in the cupboard,
And my glasses in the jam?

Always walking into rooms,
Not knowing why I'm there.
Staring at the open fridge,
A look of sheer despair.

Wondering where I've left my keys,
I hope not in the car.
Finding sugar in the salt
And thinking, 'That's bizarre.'

Stopping speaking half way through,
Forgetting what I'm saying.
Standing at the till, no longer
Sure of how I'm paying.

My slipper will be in the bin,
My phone inside my shoe.
My handbag in the garage,
And my breakfast in the loo.

The microwave's a common place,
To find things that are missing.
"Where's my feckin' drink?!" I yell,
While stomping round and hissing.

These things would happen to my mum
And secretly I'd laugh.
I'd see her standing in a daze
And think, 'She's bloody daft!'

But now this brain fog is all mine,
Confusion is my pal.
For yes - the turn is mine dear friends,
Now I'm the ditzy gal!!

Be Positive

M - make each day count, but write one off if you need to - without feeling the guilt
E - each and every one of us has something to offer; we're a force to be reckoned with
N - never say we look good for our age. We look good. Full stop
O - old age is not something we intend to slide into gracefully. We'll be screeching into it on the back of a motorbike, legs akimbo with a drink in our hands
P - power surge, not hot flush
A - age is most definitely just a number. We're young at heart, just older in other places
U - underestimate us at your peril
S - success…you're never too old. Start the new hobby, travel, write that book
E - every time you feel down, find my Facebook page. You'll have a giggle and be supported by my lovely ladies

Yes, Once we Were Young

Yes, once we were young
And now we are not.

Once we were cool
But now we are hot.

Once we could run
Not peeing our pants.
Now our wet knickers
Cause many a rant.

Our hair once was thick
And I'd say it still is.
But not where we want,
On our head it's just frizz.

It's now on our chin
Our lip and our toes.
You wouldn't believe
The places it grows.

Our belly once flat
Now definitely round.
Flap, flap, flap, flap
A regular sound.

Our manner once mild
Will rip off your head.
And sleep is no longer
For when we're in bed.

Our fanny is dry
And retired long ago.
Libido, what's that?
Does anyone know?

Our neck once a swan
Is now more a turkey.
All wrinkled and crinkled
It looks like beef jerky!!

SNOWSTORM

Bloody hell! I've just looked out of the window and seen a snow storm – in June! Oh, hang on…I sprayed my fringe with dry shampoo – while wearing my glasses…

YODA

Flush. Hot. I. Am. Having

*if Yoda was a menopausal woman

A Series of Questions

Midlife…just a series of questions:

Why did I come into this room?
Will I ever be able to sneeze without crossing my legs again?
Where did I put my glasses?
When will I grow out of the menopause?
Who decided I needed a beard?
What on earth has happened to my knees?
Why has my stomach taken on an identity of its own?
When will my hair stop appearing and disappearing from various places?

Who is brave enough to tell me how to dress?
When will society accept that midlife women are fabulous?
Where can I go on a night out to dance to 80s music?
When are we all going to realise that the world is truly our oyster?
What will happen if I stand up and do what my heart desires?
Why can't all the midlife women get together and change the world?

A Tale of Night Time

- go to bed absolutely knackered thinking, 'I'll drop to sleep the minute my head hits the pillow'.

- two hours later I'm still wide awake

- lie awake reminding myself of shopping I need and thinking of witty comebacks I should've used in that argument with a now ex-friend, two weeks ago

- finally nod off

- husband starts to snore - wakes me up

- tell him to turn onto his side, he huffs at me crossly. I manage to restrain myself from 'accidentally' kicking him, but only just

- nodding off again, realise my knickers have crept up my bum. Can I ignore them and go to sleep? No, I cannot – I persuade them back out, hubby sighs, though how he has the nerve I'll never know

- nod off again

- wake up with the first of many hot flushes. Cover off - cold - cover on and repeat - several times

- need to wee, walk to the loo effin & blinding

- get back in bed

- lie awake writing a mental list of jobs to do

- 4am nod off

- 6am hubby's alarm goes off

- manage to ignore it and doze for a bit

- cat jumps on the bed and demands attention

- other cat drinks my water from the bedside table, then playfully pushes the glass and its contents onto the floor - oh how I laugh at this playfulness…

- "FFS!" I yell while leaping out of bed to mop up the mess. Amazingly manage to stop myself from skinning the cat

- get back in bed - God loves a trier

- nod off

- next door's dog starts frantically barking - clearly someone is trapped down an old mine shaft and needs urgently rescuing

- "FML," I mutter as I give in and get up…

HRT

HRT well let's just see
If it's going to work.
I wonder where the patches
Will decide they're going to lurk.
I'll start with one stuck on my arse
And then I'll wait and see,
Where it hides, when morning comes
On hubby or on me!
Will the cat now start to grow
A pair of lovely boobs?
Or will my hubby start to sprout
A pair of luscious moobs?

Fuzzy Face

Fuzzy face
Batwing arms
Eyebrow spikes

And other charms.
Thriving beard
Nostril hair
Wrinkly pits
It's just not fair.
Scrawny neck
Sagging boobs
Drying foof
Let's get the lube.
Belly flab
Wobbly thighs
Thinning hair
And hooded eyes.
Knobbly knees
Bladder gush
Balding pubes
Or raging bush.
Sagging jowls
Hairy toes
Sleepless nights
And Flushes flow.
Murderous thoughts
Raging mouth
Our whole bod
Has headed south!!

What Day Is It?!

You know when people jokingly say they don't know what day it is? Well, when I say it, I actually mean it. I quite often wake up and for a short space of time I haven't got a bloody clue what day it is. I lie in bed running through various scenarios, until it finally dawns on me which day of the week it is. Or not.

Here are the choices:

- is hubby still in bed with me?

Yes - it's the weekend (unless his alarm's not gone off)
No - it's a week day (unless he's just gone for a wee, then it's anyone's guess)
One morning at 6.15 I woke up and was so convinced it was a work day, and there'd been an alarm malfunction, that I shook hubby awake. It was Saturday. The air was blue…

- am I feeling like I had a drink last night?

Yes - it's Saturday or Sunday (unless yesterday was a rubbish day and required alcohol, then it's anyone's guess.)
No - it's a week day

- what did I do yesterday?

And herein lies a problem because the answer to that question, no matter WHEN or WHO asks it is, "Feck knows." So, asking myself that question (as my brain thrashes around like a menopausal woman staring into a fridge wondering why her glasses, a pack of pee pads and a mug of coffee are staring back at her) is no use whatsoever

- are my work clothes hanging on the back of the door?

no - woohoo I'm not going to work! (Unless I just forgot to get them out last night) yes - the clue is in the title (unless I just hung them back up yesterday instead of putting them in the washing basket)

"AAAARRRRGGGHHHHH!

HUBBY!! WHAT BASTARD DAY IS IT??!!

Your Big End's Gone

Just had to email the garage to book the car in for an electrical fault. The reply came back saying they'll forward it to the service department and, "Sorry for the INCONTINENCE caused."

I think you'll find it's the menopause that's caused that love, not the fact that the door lock doesn't work properly!

> **GROWING UP**
> When you're a young girl you adore your mum and want to grow up to be her.
> So, nothing prepares you for the menopause hitting, looking in the mirror and discovering that in fact you've grown up to be your dad!!!

Whose Arse is This?

Let's talk about the menopausal bottom.

WHAT THE HELL HAS HAPPENED TO IT?!

I don't know about yours but mine is flabby, wobbly and yet strangely FLAT! Round, pert and firm are not words that can ever be used in the same sentence as my derrière.

I put trousers on and look ok from the front, then turn around to look at my back view in the mirror and am confronted by a flat, bulging at the sides, almost square arse! My knickers can be clearly seen struggling to pull the two cheeks back in together, "Come on lads! Work with me here, give the poor woman a break!"

Two cheeks so far apart they almost have different postcodes!

Have my glutes just given up the battle? Have they decided that holding themselves up in a rounded shape is a lost cause? Are they packing up and heading off to join my stomach, because they think it's more fun seeing where they're going rather than where they've been? Or have they just buggered off to reside on the backsides of the young and beautiful people? The lovelies who still have nicely shaped bums that sit jauntily at the tops of their legs, rather than trying to escape down the backs and round the sides of them!

Turn Around Fat Thighs…
(Based on the song *Total Eclipse of the Heart* written by Jim Steinman in 1982)

Turn around…
Every now and then I get a little bit sweaty and my fan has given up on the job

Turn around…
Every now and then I get a little bit sick of having chin hairs that refuse to come out
Turn around…
Every now and then I get a little bit sweary cos my muffin top has moved to my arse
Turn around…
Every now and then I get a little bit pissed because a turkey's taken over my neck

Turn around fat thighs
Every now and then I'm bound to fart
Turn around fat thighs
Every now and then I'll fall apart

Turn around…
Every now and then I get a little bit hairy but my nether regions now are just bald
Turn around…
Every now and then I get a little bit cross because my glasses seem to hide in the bin
Turn around…
Every now and then I get a little bit panicked when I need the loo but nothing's in sight
Turn around…
Every now and then I get a little bit arsey cos my mirror's clearly telling a lie

Turn around fat thighs
Every now and then I'm bound to fart
Turn around fat thighs
Every now and then I'll fall apart…

Welcome to the Madhouse

Welcome to the madhouse, the funhouse, the damp and sweaty hot house
The fat house, the frizzy house, the 'it's all gone to pot' house.
The sore house, the fart house, the balding or the hairy house
The itchy house, the angry house, the sometimes very sweary house.
The tired house, the acne house, the scarily forgetful house
The bloated house, the manic house, the 'everything is stressful' house.
The leaky house, the dried-up house, the 'don't look in the mirror' house
The twitchy house, the bitchy house, the 'best not get too near her' house.
The anxious house, the grumpy house, the 'I think you'd better duck' house
The tearful house, the fearful house, the 'I do not give a fuck' house.

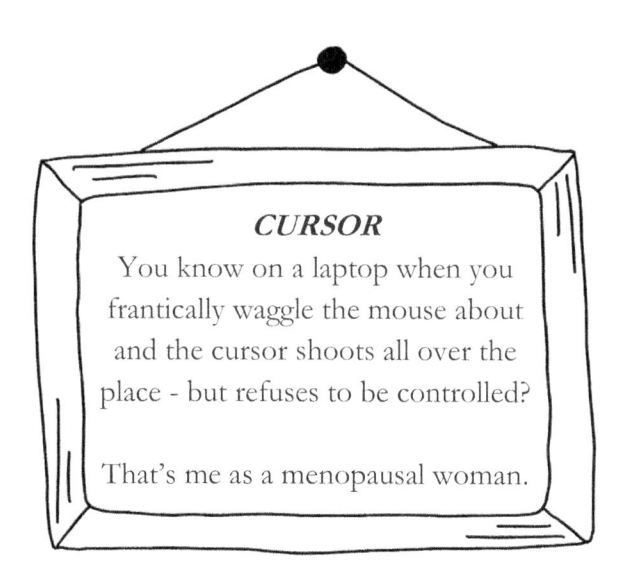

CURSOR

You know on a laptop when you frantically waggle the mouse about and the cursor shoots all over the place - but refuses to be controlled?

That's me as a menopausal woman.

The Sweary Menopause

FFS! I'm melting!

Here comes a BASTARD sneeze!

You are so FECKIN' annoying!

My hair's like TWATTING straw!

BOLLOCKS! What was I saying?!

Where's this BUGGERING fat come from?!

Has it Gone, or Is It Coming Back?

Remember when they finally stop?
You freeze and then your stomach drops.
So, do I need to buy a pram
Or has the meno built a dam?

You've spent a while with random dates
Have they gone, or am I late?
Have they petered out to zero?
Is the meno now my hero?

Until the symptoms then appear
And everything becomes so clear.
It's not a bun being cooked inside
It's welcome to the meno ride.

No need to pee upon a stick
A crib, a pram, and clothes to pick.
The only thing I'll have to nurse
Is the feckin dreaded meno curse!

PHEW!

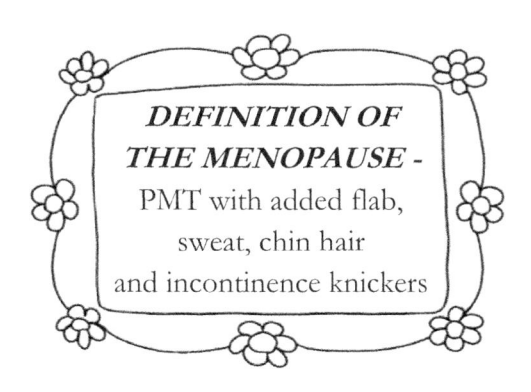

> **DEFINITION OF THE MENOPAUSE -**
> PMT with added flab, sweat, chin hair and incontinence knickers

What if Evil Step-Mothers were Simply Menopausal?

What if all the evil step-mothers in fairy tales weren't actually evil. What if they were just menopausal?

Perhaps they'd had enough of dealing with hot flushes and rogue muffin tops and couldn't be arsed to help lure in a passing, unwitting Prince Charming for their tiresome, beautiful step-daughter. A step-daughter who wafts around all day with dewy skin, perfectly made-up eyes and rosebud lips. How dare she wake up looking absolutely gorgeous, as opposed to looking like a swamp monster whose face is so creased even an iron would run away screaming.

Maybe Cinderella had to scrub the kitchen floor because her step-mother's joints were aching and the constant jerking forward of the mop was causing her to wet herself. Tena hadn't been invented then and I'm not sure a cast-off bit of breeches would've been up to the job.

What if Hansel and Gretel were pissing off their step-mother, who'd had enough of their constant demands for attention, when all she wanted to do was have a gin, a box of chocolates, some peace and a nana nap.

In Sleeping Beauty, the evil step-mother has morphed into a withered old bag of a fairy, who is furious about not being invited to a good old knees up. Don't antagonise a menopausal woman because they've had enough of being treated as if they were invisible - and if you don't invite them, they might just rock up anyway. And then go full on nuclear at your audacity, when they arrive.

And could it have been brain fog that caused the evil step-mother to offer Snow White a poisoned apple? Maybe she was just confused and thought she was at a Halloween party offering an apple for a lovely game of apple bobbing. Perhaps the poison within the apple was to help deal with a rat infestation in the castle and she'd merely picked up the wrong one.

In another story she's morphed into an evil witch responsible for locking Rapunzel up in a tower. Well, she probably just couldn't stand hoovering up Rapunzel's twatting hair anymore, because the girl was shedding like a bloody Labrador on heat!

Muesli

Muesli…the piss pad of the cereal world… soaks up liquid and expands when wet.

Don't get them mixed up though…one dried up thing in your knickers is bad enough without having oat flakes, sultanas and nuts dropping out of them all day.

Being brought down by a pack of squirrels, wanting to chomp on your underwear, is rather unseemly to say the least!

The Menopausal Fart

I'm afraid I didn't see you there
When I let one rip without a care.
My menopausal arse now large
Can't stop them when they freely charge.
The little buggers can be frisky
Which does make bending rather risky.
I cross the room to beating drums
The percussion coming from my bum.
The cat must think it's quite alarming.

And looks as if to say, "That's charming!"
I mount the stairs with turbo power
And ping them out when in the shower.
I gaily trumpet as I walk
It's almost like my arse now talks.
This excess wind is one more thing
The menopause does kindly bring.
The National Grid should harness me
Along with barges on the sea!
No turbine powered electricity
Just check my knicks' elasticity!

Dry eyes??!!

What the buggery bollox is that all about??!!

My eyes now gush as enthusiastically as my bladder, every time I step foot outside the house!

Guess what…turns out it's a menopause symptom…of course it is.

Apparently, your eyes dry out - like other parts of your anatomy - so to compensate for this Sahara Desert situation your eyeballs decide to excrete liquid out of them faster than your clothes can shrink a size overnight.

I walk to work and arrive with smudged mascara and streaky foundation, due to the constant rivulets of eye juice that have poured down my cheeks for the entire journey.

Do we not suffer enough?!

I can't believe we now have to stick pee pads to our feckin eyes!

Pull 'Em Up!

Pull you pants up nice and high
To your tum and round your thigh.
Tuck in any straddling hair
Then off you go without a care.
Our bellies now are hard to tame
Our shape from us they've truly claimed.
Big knickers are our last resort
To try and make our bellies taut.
But failing that just let it hang
Try not to feel a mournful pang
Ask it nicely, belly please…
Do not hang around our knees!

It's Friday!

Bingo wings and drooping boobs
Dried up foof and balding pubes
Piss pad wedged inside our knicks
Thinning line around our lips
Tash that's lush and bearded chin
Eyebrows white and getting thin
Muffin top that's taking charge
Knickers now extremely large
It's Friday though, so we will grin
And pour ourselves a massive gin!!

Dear Menopause,

I understand about depleting hormones making my stomach rounder and fuller than I'd like. I get it.

But my arms too?

Why the hell have my upper arms swollen to the point where my sleeves take them hostage, cut off their blood supply and convince me that I'LL NEVER GET THAT TOP OFF AGAIN!!

Sort yourself out please.

Yours,
Bloated of Barnsley

We Wear the Damp Pants
(Based on the song *We Are the Champions written by Freddie Mercury in 1977*)

We've paid our dues
We've done our time
First periods then meno
It feels like a crime.
We stand up to it all
Cos women are strong
Once middle-aged we won't take your crap
So don't do us wrong!!!

And we mean to go on and on and on and on

Cos we wear the damp pants my friends
And we'll keep on fighting till the end

We wear the damp pants
We wear the damp pants
No time for snoozes
Cos we wear the damp pants of the world.

We've taken our bows
And tried not to fall
Chin hairs and flab
We've suffered it all.
We're sick of your nonsense
You've made us quite bored
We refuse to be invisible
No longer ignored!!!

And we mean to go on and on and on and on

Cos we wear the damp pants my friends
And we'll keep on fighting till the end
We wear the damp pants
We wear the damp pants
No time for snoozes
Cos we wear the damp pants of the world.

> **THE MENOPAUSE**
> Going through life one
> chin hair at a time...

Sharon the Showgirl
(Based on the song *Copacabana* written by Barry Manilow in 1985)

Her name was Sharon, she was a showgirl
With a menopausal twist and I think
you get the gist
She would merengue and do the cha cha
And while she wore her piss pad well
It would often really swell.

She'd samba one to four
And find the toilet door
She'd burst in with legs crossed tight
Before she wet…the…floor!!!

Meno Queen
(Based on the song Dancing Queen written bu Benny Andersson, Bjorn Ulvaeus and Stig Anderson for Abba in 1976)

You can dance…you can jive
Wearing a piss pad or five
Ooh, see that girl, old and keen
Digging the meno queen.

Friday night and the lights are low
Muffin top under firm control.
Where they play the right music, getting in the swing
You come to look for a gin.

Anybody could be that pissed
Night is young and the mouth is missed
With a bit of rock music - and a glass of wine

You're in the mood for a dance.
And when you get the chance…

You are the meno queen
Two left feet, chin hairs long and preened
Meno queen
Feel the squeeze from your too tight jeans, oh yeah

You can dance…you can jive
Wearing a piss pad or five
Ooh, see that girl, old and keen
Digging the meno queen.

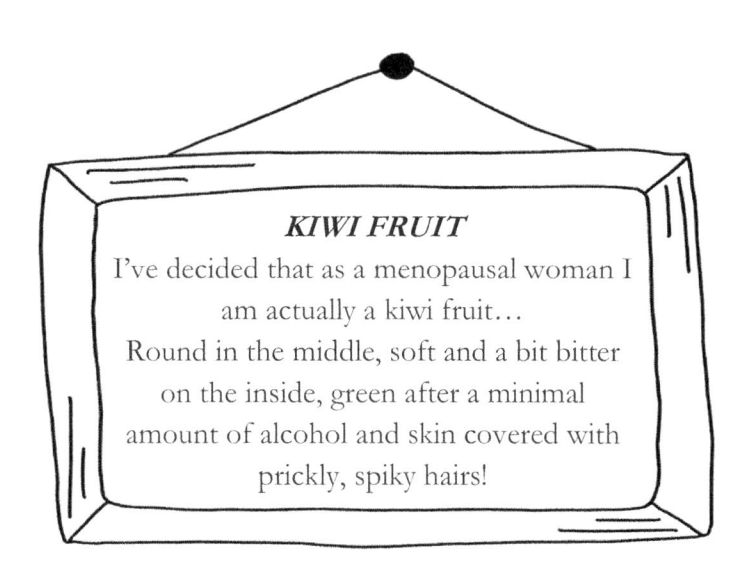

KIWI FRUIT
I've decided that as a menopausal woman I am actually a kiwi fruit…
Round in the middle, soft and a bit bitter on the inside, green after a minimal amount of alcohol and skin covered with prickly, spiky hairs!

MENO, MENO

Meno, meno give me your answer do,
I'm half crazy
Over the things you do…
It won't be a stylish marriage
The state of my undercarriage
With dried up bits
Plus hairy tits
And a muffin top built for two!

THE BERMUDA TRIANGLE

Menopause – the Bermuda Triangle of midlife.
Responsible for the disappearance of your sleep, your mind, your waistline and your bladder control!!

SWEARING

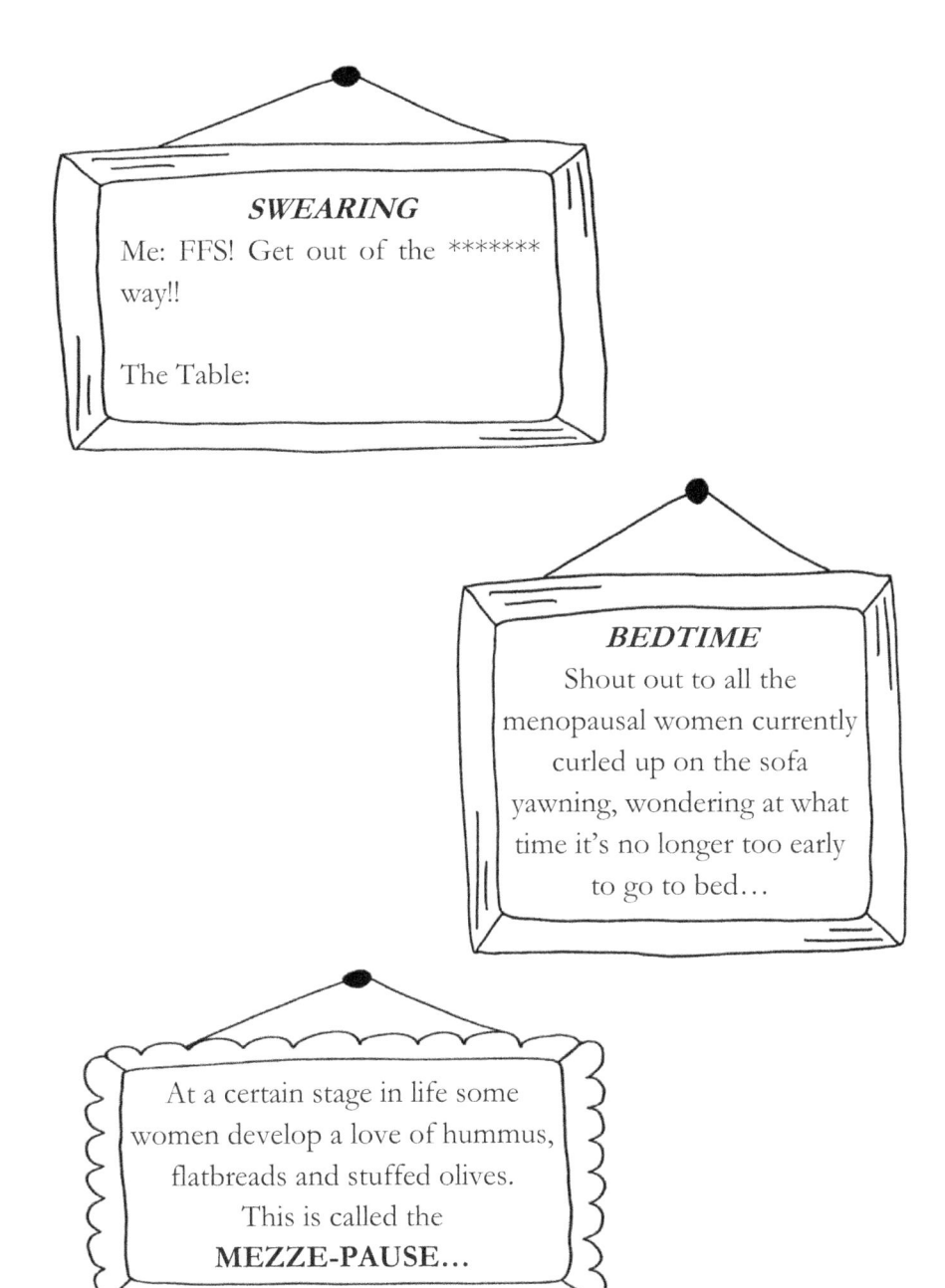

Me: FFS! Get out of the ******* way!!

The Table:

BEDTIME

Shout out to all the menopausal women currently curled up on the sofa yawning, wondering at what time it's no longer too early to go to bed…

At a certain stage in life some women develop a love of hummus, flatbreads and stuffed olives. This is called the
MEZZE-PAUSE…

THIS IS HOW IT ENDS

Ageing is a Gift

Hello there, lovely ladies
   Come right in and take a seat.
   The mirror's where we're going to look,
Yourself you're going to greet.

We'll start up at the top I think,
I feel that's for the best.
We'll take in all the things we see
The worst, and all the rest.

Hair that's thinning or is frizzy
Lost its colour and its style.
Sends us searching for new products
Down the lying, haircare aisle.

Eyebrows greying, or with balding bits
Or bushy by degrees.
But all of them have long, white hairs
That daily need a tweeze.

Our face no more a smooth, young peach
Or lovely shiny pear.
It's turned into a kiwi skin

With stubborn, spikey hairs!

A neck to make a turkey proud
No matter what we try.
Exercise and special creams
"The crepe's still there!" we sigh.

Loose and saggy armpit skin
And dreaded bingo wings.
We wave our arms, they laugh at us
As in the breeze they swing.

Our boobs will droop or sag or flop
Or simply sit there flat.
Yet nipples strangely now protrude -
A good place for a hat!

The stomach, well what's here to stay
It's flabby now, our belly.
It hangs above our knickers
Like a happy, wobbly jelly.

Our nether regions now are bald
Or a wild untended mess.
Which means it either gets tucked in
Or sits like spaced out cress!

Our knees are just like two old men
Who grin without their teeth.
With oddly sprouting, wiry hair
On their faces and beneath.

And wrapped around our lower legs
Are blue and knotty lines.

That look like dried and wrinkled grapes
On twisted, ancient vines.

Our toes look like they should belong
On hobbits from the woods.
I'm tempted now to take them back
As damaged, faulty goods!

But ladies look at what's inside
Our ageing, changing shell.
And think about the things we've done
And how we've done them well.

We've gone through life, met challenges
We've cried and had a hoot.
We've worked, we've cared, we've organised
And this we should salute.

So, grab your friends and family
And let the ageing happen.
Support and love each other
Cos our strength is our best weapon.

Go out and age the way you want
Don't start to feel adrift.
Embrace the changes, every one
Cos aging is a gift.

ACKNOWLEDGEMENTS

I would like to take this chance to publicly thank Yvonne Vincent and Mr V.

Yvonne is a very successful author (*Losers Club*) and Facebook blogger (*Growing Old Disgracefully*). She and her husband have led me by the hand into the world of self-publishing. They both gave freely and generously of their time to get me to this point and I seriously could not - and would not - have done it without them both.

My husband Doug needs a mention for proof reading my ramblings, jokingly declaring a lot of them as "Pure filth" but laughing and supporting my writing endeavours anyway.

Thank you to my two sons, Alistair and Stewart, for not being too embarrassed by what I've written and for encouraging me to keep going.

And last, but not least, a massive thank you to all of my extremely supportive Facebook followers who encouraged me to write a book by constantly telling me that I have a talent, a gift for writing and a way with words. You are responsible for me finally taking the plunge.

Only you, dear reader, can decide if my followers were speaking the truth or talking absolute buggery bollox. I'm hoping for the former xx

AFTERWORD

Look out for my next book *More Midlife Dramas in Pyjamas* to be published soon.

This next book covers things like battles with technology, health issues, being a woman and trying to keep fit – amongst other topics. Here's a sneak peek from the chapter: Nursery Rhymes Aren't Just for Children

Mary Had a Little Lamb

Mary had a little lamb
With less hair than her muff.
"I need to see a specialist
To sort out my wee chuff!"

So off she went to see the girl
And said, "I beg your pardon
I think you'll need the mower, love
To sort MY lady garden!"

You can find me here:

Facebook: @midlifedramasinpyjamas
Instagram: @midlifedramasinpyjamas
www.etsy.com/shop/mdipcreations

Printed in Dunstable, United Kingdom